Empathy

Empathy

Hoa Pham

Goldsmiths
Press

A CIP record for this book is available from the British Library

ISBN 978-1-913380-61-8 (pbk)
ISBN 978-1-913380-60-1 (ebk)

www.gold.ac.uk/goldsmiths-press

Goldsmiths
UNIVERSITY OF LONDON

For Alister, Max and William for sharing my true empathy.

Hanoi – Vuong

We have always been we. Then they forced us to become you and I.

When I was a little girl, I would look in the bathroom mirror to reassure myself I was not alone. The girl in the mirror smiled at we when I smiled at her. We would press against the mirror with our hands and all I would feel was the cold surface against my skin.

I learnt quickly not to tell the Department about what I did, nor to reveal anything to the lady who thought she was being kind by visiting and reassuring we. Occasionally I thought of telling one of the other foster children. Exchanging secrets made you friends. But I didn't need friends with we hiding behind the mirror. And besides, I could not rely on other people not to give me away.

Today I look in the mirror and know that despite my lover Camille I am truly alone. I put on make-up, though I'm not sure why. The taste of the lipstick and hint of perfume make me feel adult. Today, when I finally meet we, I'm anxious and full of trepidation. It's been twenty years and what I have longed for is coming true.

My curiosity abounded when they told me I could finally meet her – under the watchful eye of the Department. The

Department had brought me up with other foster children in Việt Nam. They gave me food and shelter, and schooling. We were the privileged ones, we were told. In the compound you could go to university if you were smart and knew what to tell them.

I did not tell them that I was missing my multiple eyes. They punish you for thinking about we instead of me. So I learnt to hide it at an early age and the phantoms of my sisters kept me company in that enforced solitude.

Now finally I was about to meet one of them again after twenty years.

This morning I had worried over my appearance. I didn't want her to think that I was one of them, that I was the Department. But I knew I would be searched, and I had to seem to be one of them in order to access her.

I had bad dreams the night before. About being angry, hiding under a table and being yelled at by monitors. When I had woken up, sweating, I was doubly aware of the camera in the corner of my flat that watched me as I slept. Camille was fast asleep by my side. She did not sleep lightly.

I had never been to a rehabilitation centre before. The barbed-wire fences were imposing and during the strip-search I pretended I was at my regular medical check-up. The monitor sent with me was searched too, and that reassured me. Her name was Evelyn, an English Vietnamese-speaking researcher for the Department. She dressed casually, in jeans and a white shirt.

"I will come in with you and then leave you alone," Evelyn assured me.

The steady wink-wink of the security cameras following me told the lie, as did the green identity bracelet they snapped around my wrist.

The detention centre was modern with stark pale-green walls and metal doors.

When we passed the first round of security and were in the inner wing, I felt a stare on my face. I looked up and one of the guards, dressed in black, was taking in my dress.

"I'm her sister," I said.

They wanted us to be treated as normal citizens. The guards and staff were not told officially that we were multiples, but I was sure word would get out. That Việt Nam had succeeded in cloning was the biggest open secret in the world. Most of the Western world had said it was fake news, and overseas we were considered quintuplets rather than clones.

The guard snapped to attention at Evelyn's discreet cough and escorted us into the secured ward.

"We want what's best for Lien," Evelyn said to me as we walked down the detention-green corridors. "She is a sick woman."

I nodded, trying to seem calm and ignoring the tension in my stomach. I was so nervous I wanted to throw up. I had only seen her picture before they took me here, and that night I had looked in the mirror tracing the contours of my cheeks with my fingers.

Dark lacquer eyes, dark hair and the same cheekbones. We were multiples and yet the expression on her face haunted me the most. It was of horror and shock.

I didn't want to meet a murderer.

But I wanted to see my multiple sister who had been company for so long. Other children had imaginary friends. I knew my multiples were not imaginary. They just weren't physically there with me.

Be prepared for disappointment, Evelyn had told me in the car. She's not like you.

Not like we.

I wanted to feel connected again. I wasn't allowed to tell my colleagues where I was going – all my life I had had to hide my true nature from the world. Now, finally, I was allowed to admit it, in rehabilitation.

Was the rehabilitation for her or me?

I did not know. I was clever and they knew it. I did well at school and was accelerated into university.

Just standing next to Evelyn made me ill. I had pretended I was normal until I saw that picture. I thought I had adapted to the world I was supposed to live in. I was a success. But now…

I hated Evelyn then as she let the guard open the door to where Lien was staying.

"Lien." Evelyn's voice was deceptively neutral. "Vuong is here to see you."

Evelyn gestured for me to come forward.

I walked into the padded cell under the glare of the fluorescent lights.

Sitting on the couch, Lien was hunched over, her black fringe hiding her face. She was dressed in the blue denim of the rehabilitation centre and suddenly she looked directly at me. I was fixed by her gaze and I stared back into eyes that mirrored my own.

We.

The door closed behind me and I flinched. I knew we were to be left alone, but this girl had murdered her foster father with her bare hands.

Tears welled up in her eyes. She threw her arms around me, clinging, and I held her back. I found myself crying too.

Suddenly we were back there, and I was no longer me, I was a multiple with my sister. We then touched palms together and she smiled.

"Are the others coming?" she asked, and my throat closed.

"I don't know."

"I dream of we. All the time. I want to see the others. They can't have all turned out as good-looking as you."

I laughed, and I heard the strain in my own voice. She was identical to me and the irony did not escape her. There was a glint in her eye that I recognised from my own watchfulness. In the corner was the camera, recording, recording for prosperity what we did and said for the Department. We were unique, and we were multiple.

"I was told," I said carefully, "that I could see you first. Then they don't know."

"Ah." Something settled in her eyes and I knew that her stare, smiling, wondering, was reflected by mine.

"I'm the bad one," she said ruefully, and I laughed again. "But what he did was wrong." Her words shocked me back to reality. I was in a rehabilitation centre. Killing was wrong. "Have you seen the others?"

"No." It was the truth.

She could not stop smiling and we embraced like multiples again. Then reluctantly she stepped back, still holding my hand.

"They do not like us showing affection," she said, looking at the camera over my shoulder.

"I know," I said.

She sat back on the couch and I sat on the bed.

"Have you come to take me out of here? Be my sponsor?" The hope in her eyes devastated me.

"No. They… don't want us to be together. They want me to just talk to you. They thought… that perhaps I could make you feel better." The false words, the Department's words, dropped like stones from my mouth. I hoped she could not see the lie in them. "They want to understand why you did what you did. To make sure the other multiples do not do the same. Somehow with all their batteries of tests and rehabilitation they have not understood."

"You make me feel better just being here. I've been good so they let me see one of we."

She started to cry again and this time I initiated the hug. Lien was so ground down by the Department she had slipped up and called us "we." Maybe this was what they wanted to do to her. Break her.

"Is your monitor good?" she asked. "She seems nice. She visited me a couple of times before she told me she monitored you."

"She's all right." I said. I did not want to admit that I was rarely monitored nowadays, that I was the healthy one.

"The monitors here are kind. They wouldn't make us eat… meat. Everyone in rehab is so different and the monitors just accept us the way we are. There are some real weird ones in here though."

My nerves pricked up when she mentioned meat. She had eaten pork before killing her foster father. Evelyn had told me that the foster father had a clean record as a farmer. It was eating the pork that had catalysed her, that had tipped her over the edge. At least that was the reasoning that she gave to the Department.

I ate meat on the odd special occasion. I preferred eating rice and fish. Evelyn commented that neither of us multiples had explored much in the way of food choices once we were exposed to the outside world. We stuck to what we knew.

Repetition did not scare we. Change did.

"Do they know you are a multiple?"

Her eyes shifted to the camera. "The staff know. They told me… that they wouldn't tell the others. I think some of them might suspect… But we don't talk about the past here. We talk about the future, what we're going to become."

The Department mantra coming from Lien's mouth without a hint of irony frightened me. I looked into her lacquer-deep eyes and she smiled, stirring something inside me. The bond was intense, hypnotic.

I didn't want to fall prey to it. I wanted to be able to walk away from here. But something essential to me was filled by holding Lien's trusting hand – I was a multiple of a killer. At least that was what the Department told me.

"What do you do?" she asked, and her keen curiosity frightened me, paralysed me. She wanted to know everything, like we did. But I had adjusted too well, and I could not share everything. I wanted to be I, not we. I did not want to kill.

"I'm a psychology researcher."

Her eyes shifted to the camera. "You aren't here to study me, are you? You need an ethics clearance for that."

"No!" Her suspicion cut me to the quick. I wanted to do well by her. "I'm your designated next of kin. After your father... died..."

"You don't need to dance around it. I know he died. I know I did it. I have reason for what we did."

Her hand squeezed mine and I wanted to back away.

"Lien, I didn't kill your father. We are not we anymore."

This basic lesson, hammered into us when they released us, made her face crumple for a moment. Then she straightened up and let go of my hand. When she turned her gaze to me again she was cool and distant.

The sudden retreat from our intimacy left me stranded in the rehab room. I glanced at the camera and remembered why I was there.

"I know what my rights are now," she said softly. "And yours. I know you are different. They told me you were different from me. The Department raised you. At least I had a family."

I took a step back from her.

"Hurting me isn't going to get you out of here, Lien. And you had a family. Why did you kill him?" I asked her directly. I wanted out of the room.

"He made me eat pig."

"Is that a good enough reason for killing him?" Evelyn had told me she had attacked him. She spared me the details.

"The pigs were we," she said simply. I stared at her aghast. Had she bonded with all the pigs? "There were many of them. All the same. They were like we. And he killed them!" She started crying again, noisily.

This time I didn't touch her. Was it my job to reason with her?

I looked at the door. It remained closed. Then I stared at the camera. The red light winked at me. They were watching. They knew. They weren't going to let me out.

"The pigs aren't we," I said softly and touched her hand. Again that shock of feeling linked me with her. She stopped crying suddenly like a tap. I had the feeling she had been crying for a long time and she was exhausted.

That was why they wanted me here. To remind her of her multiple nature. Her human nature.

And to remind me.

Her intent stare did not unnerve me this time. Instead I shared her stare, my mirror image. I could have killed. I could have murdered a human being. But I had not.

That was what made me *me*.

"Pigs are animals," I said and she frowned. "Killing humans is wrong." I stopped myself from completing the logical conclusion. Killing animals for food is all right. But I couldn't tell her that. She clearly disagreed.

You can't show the same empathy to animals as humans and survive. Not in Việt Nam, anyway.

Behind me the door opened.

Automatically we stopped holding hands and faced Evelyn.

"What did we learn today?" Evelyn asked and the ritual monitoring question made we want to throttle her.

"We are not we. The pigs… are not we," Lien said like an obedient doll.

"And Vuong?"

My suspicions bloomed. This was an intervention for me too. I wondered what I had done to need a monitoring lesson.

"She is not me," I said as if I was five years old again.

"You can say goodbye now. Vuong will come again."

I would?

Lien embraced me but we did not press cheek to cheek. Instead we stood a healthy distance apart, the way we had for all those monitors all those years ago.

"I look forward to seeing you again, Vuong. Thank you, Evelyn." Lien politely bowed her head, and I knew the civility she wore was a mask.

My mask almost slipped as I left her alone in that padded cell.

I am free. And she is not me.

"You will see her again," Evelyn told me. "She's very difficult to reason with. It is the first time she has identified herself away from the pigs to us. She's a vegan and believes that animals are we. So she killed her father in retaliation. We don't know why she suddenly objected to eating pork. I didn't want you to push her too far."

I frowned, gazing at Evelyn, wondering if she had been one of the many monitors that were assigned solely to we.

"Will I get to see the others?"

"We'll see." Evelyn escorted me out of the rehabilitation centre, her attention elsewhere.

I chewed on my lip as we walked out of the inner wing, oblivious to the stares of the guards upon me. I wanted to curl up in a foetal ball and cry, like I did when I was five and was told we were going to be split and brought up away from each other.

It was wrong that Lien was in rehab. Instinctively I knew what she meant by the pigs being we. They cloned animals too, identical animals.

"What do you think of her?" Evelyn asked after we were strip-searched again and escorted out into the car park.

I looked at Evelyn and the tears we had shed in front of their mechanical eyes must have shown on my face. "Don't make her eat meat." Evelyn nodded as we got into her car to drive me back to the flats.

"How do you feel?" she asked me before starting the ignition.

"Upset. I'll come again to visit her. She shouldn't be alone."

I shouldn't be alone, my thoughts echoed, but I did not tell the monitor that.

Evelyn drummed her fingers against the steering wheel.

The Department did not really care about we. They wanted us to be healthy individuals.

All the old resentments that I thought I had put away from my childhood rose in me again. It was because of Departmental largesse that Lien was in a rehabilitation centre.

She would not have killed or thought the pigs were we if we had been there to remind her.

But I had to co-operate with Evelyn.

I wanted to see the others.

I wanted to be we again.

Berlin – My

Sometimes I just sat on the windowsill of our apartment and felt the wind against my skin. I looked down at the busy straight-line streets, at the fractures that were Berlin, and wondered at the fissures gaping under there.

History was present in the concrete and tourists took pictures of what used to divide us. Though I was a born German, I was also Vietnamese, and this difference made me a stranger.

My friends were few and far between. Perhaps I was too picky, too untrusting. But most people looked at me oddly when I asked them whether they had ever thought that there was more to life than this shift, than this café. Certainly there seemed to be no more to my mother's life; she had worked the same night-time cleaning shift for thirty years at the CHESS chemical factory in East Berlin, she had her regular weekly meeting, the hui circle, her only group of friends.

But there was more to it, as I soon found out.

When I first met Truong, he was a customer at the pho restaurant where I worked. We also sold sushi and pad thai, servicing all Asian cuisines like all Asian restaurants in West Berlin. I noticed him because of his fingers tapping to Massive Attack playing on the restaurant stereo. He was cute, with a ponytail and snug black leather jacket and black jeans.

When he saw me looking at his long fingers playing the rhythm he smiled.

"Massive Attack. I saw them last month," he commented.

"Me too," I said.

"I recorded their concert. You can download it from my site for a small fee," he told me. He plucked out his wallet and handed me a glossy business card with a name – Truong Nguyen – and website.

"Cool, thanks." I fetched his pho, đặc biệt special with offal and all the trimmings.

"I'm Truong by the way."

"My."

"Nice to meet you."

The restaurant got busy then, and he ate his pho while I worked. I observed him out of the corner of my eye. He caught me at it, and winked as he ensnared my gaze with a smile.

I grew warm under his scrutiny, pleasantly so.

Before he left he smiled at me again and said goodbye.

I liked how he kept his distance and gave me the means to access him without asking for an e-mail or site in return. His circumspection made me respect him more.

I did not think I was that attractive, though I had double-pierced my ears to break with people's assumptions that I was just a good Vietnamese daughter working in the restaurant.

Occasionally a lovesick traditional Vietnamese boy would make eyes at me while I cleaned tables. Subservience was attractive to them, and when I showed them lip it scared them right away.

My mother wanted me to get a nice Vietnamese boyfriend. I did not think she meant a bootlegger with a ponytail.

I headed upstairs to our apartment, went to my bedroom and plugged in my laptop.

The website on his card was for a network of market stalls around Berlin selling bootlegs of CDs and DVDs. A contact e-mail and a mobile number scrolled underneath the ever-changing graphics of the front page.

There was an impressive catalogue of concert recordings from the last three years. Curious, I tapped on the one for Massive Attack. The quality was tinny but my laptop speakers could have been to blame. The sample was of my favourite song, "Girl."

I tapped on the e-mail address and my browser opened up.

Then my phone beeped.

A text from my best friend wanting to go to Berghain tonight.

Smiling, I got ready to leave the apartment and go out.

Standing in the turnstile queue I jiggled up and down, my breath puffing steam. Freja cuddled herself in her purple fur-lined jacket and I pulled my black hood over my hair. My cheeks were like ice. The clubbers around us were in jeans or stockings with long boots. The queue shuffled forward as security frisked us for weapons or booze. After paying the admission I gladly walked into the greenhouse atmosphere of the club and shed my hoodie and scarf.

"So where's this man, Mattias?" I asked Freja, who flicked back her bright matchstick-red hair.

"Around somewhere."

"Did he just tell you to meet here at 12?"

"Not in this spot exactly. At Berghain."

I stilled my tongue at her stupidity. Berghain was a converted power station with five floors of clubbing. Meeting here without a specific spot was like saying you would meet at Ostbahnhof, near the trains somewhere.

But that was Freja. She took more risks than I did and knew how to look out for herself. She probably didn't even have his mobile number.

"Let's dance." Freja grinned at me, and as always I forgave her.

We pushed our way through the crowded ground floor and climbed the stairs, where UV lights picked out teeth and the stitching on people's jeans. Heading to the second floor I slid the metallic neon bangles up my wrists, frippery I did not wear during the daytime.

The bass beats pulsed through my sneakers and I lost myself in the rhythms, happy to be part of the heaving masses. Berghain was for serious dancing – picking up occurred in the toilets and Berghain was a well-known beat. So long as you didn't look too closely at what you were sitting on or what was going on in the nearby vicinity, nobody would bother you.

It was hard to believe that during the first lockdowns Berghain had been used as a plant nursery when it could not be a dance club. Now, surrounded by punters drinking and dancing, it was as if the pandemic had never happened.

I left Freja to get drinks from the bar. When I came back, two Red Bulls and two shooters in hand, she was no longer there. After a cursory exploration of the floor I sat down on the concrete and poured myself a Jägerbomb. She would text me if she needed or wanted to find me.

Tossing it down, I bobbed my head in time to the bass. Then to my astonishment I recognised the young man leaning up against the wall next to me.

"Gute Nacht!" I said, raising an empty glass to him.

The ponytailed bootlegger squatted down next to me. His eyes were clear and as far as I could tell he was sober.

"Would you like a drink?" I gestured at the makings in front of me.

"I'll have the Red Bull but not that." He handed the Jägermeister back to me.

"You sure?" The alcohol was making my cheeks warm.

"I don't drink," he said and my respect for him went up another notch.

Then I tossed back the Jägermeister. I didn't have class tomorrow morning, I wasn't going anywhere.

"Who are you here with?" he asked, gazing at the dancing, jumping crowd.

"I was here with my best friend but she went off to meet a man." As I said the words my native caution set in. But I could not sense any danger or even a special interest in me.

"I'm here with my old school friends. They're in there somewhere." He gestured at the mass of bodies. I noticed he was bopping to the music ever so slightly. He probably didn't even realise he was doing it.

"I liked the samples on your webpage," I said. " 'Girl' is my favourite song."

He grinned and our eyes met with a surge of energy. I told myself it wasn't just the booze. When he smiled I realised he was handsome.

"It's mine too. I love how at their concerts they put up damning stats about the world. It's not just trip hop, it's got meaning." Truong smiled at me again. He was a boy with a social conscience. Immediately I showed more interest.

"Wanna dance?" I asked.

"I don't usually pick up at clubs," he told me as I nestled in the crook of his arm.

"Neither do I," I admitted.

"You must get hit on at the pho shop."

"I do. Usually when I answer back in German it scares the little critters away."

He laughed.

"So how come you're available?" he asked.

"My last relationship came to a sticky end. He left me for an older French woman. Said she was more sophisticated." Truong snorted. "And you?"

"She wanted a relationship… and I didn't know what one was."

"What do you think it is?"

"I know what it isn't. My father hit my mother when he was drunk. Would call her names. It's why I don't drink. I'm not going to be like that bastard."

"Wow." I sat in silence for a moment. "I hardly see my mother – she goes to work when I go to bed and vice versa." I was running at the mouth, I had said so much. But 3am drunk at Berghain was the time for confidences. And for deciding if I was going to go to bed with him.

"At least you're at uni. Prime time for not knowing what you're doing."

"Why aren't you?" I asked him. He was obviously intelligent and streetwise.

"Don't know. I've had other things to do. I worry… German uni students don't have parents working in factories."

I crossed my legs thinking about that.

"I know what you mean. They don't work in factories either. But it's not too bad once you've found one or two people to relate to."

"Yeah. I found you…" he said bravely and I moved in for a kiss.

"Hey, Truong! Truong!"

I felt a gentle shove on the shoulder and I woke up entwined with Truong on a tattered couch, still at Berghain. Three guys, two Asian and one German, were bouncing around us. Truong looked dazed and confused but extricated himself, still holding my hand.

"Can't leave you alone for… oh, two hours," the German joked.

"This is My." Truong introduced me. "Van, Toby and Michael."

I blinked at them.

"Let's have one more dance and get some pho," Van said.

His German scraped my ears and I recognised his accent as Southern Vietnamese. Truong had a mix of friends – like many of us second-generation he didn't differentiate by Vietnamese geography.

Early in the morning and Berghain had not let up. People were still streaming in and we descended to the first floor. Belatedly I checked my phone and as I had predicted Freja had found her man and stranded me alone.

But I wasn't alone.

Truong opened out the palm of his hand and offered me a choice of pink heart-shaped lollies. He took two and swallowed, then gestured for me to do the same.

"Empathy. Pure grade," he mouthed at me.

Shrugging, I swallowed the pills. I had heard of empathy, it was supposed to make you hyper-sensitive and hyper-high. First time for everything, I thought, entrusting myself to a near stranger.

We started dancing and the four of them moved together in the same way. I tried to copy them but realised that the footwork was beyond me after what I had drunk and taken. Berghain was steaming and Truong took off his shirt, tucking it into the back pocket of his jeans. Under the UV light his dragon tattoo writhed with his movements and its scales winked silver and white. The dragon's body spread across his chest, the head nestling in the hollow of his shoulder.

"Cool tattoo," I mouthed at him and he smiled. Expensive and painful, I thought to myself, watching his body ripple.

In the back of my mind, the thought that he might be part of the Vietnamese mafia briefly surfaced and then was dismissed. My mother would not be impressed, but I wasn't going out with her.

The dance track morphed into trance music and the boys stopped dancing in sync. Truong casually moved in towards me and put his hands around my waist. Enclosed by the dragon, I kissed its tongue with my lips. I felt a flicker in my mouth and then the sensation was gone, leaving me wondering.

We emerged from Berghain as the sun was coming up, a pink highlight on the horizon. Shivering at the cold change, I let Truong wrap me up in his bomber jacket.

"Let's catch a cab back to the East." Van said. "The best pho is in the East," he teased me.

"Have you tried the pho in Kreuzberg?" I asked him as we jiggled up and down on the spot in the queue waiting for a cab.

"I have," Toby volunteered. "Sweeter."

"Egg," Van said and slapped him on the back good-humouredly. Egg – yellow on the inside, white on the out-side. Toby was the token white guy in their four-set, and had been since grade 8 at school.

We bundled ourselves into the cab and Truong put his arm protectively around me. I put my hand on his chest where the dragon was. I could feel the serpentine body rippling under my fingers.

The cab drove into East Berlin. Outside the apartments were stark and modernist, grey in the dawn. Street-sweepers went by and the occasional car.

We hopped out of the cab at three steel aircraft hangars, all in a row, in a vast car park. The Dong Ma complex, the heart of Vietnamese commerce.

"This way." Truong held my hand.

We walked up to a hangar and Michael opened the door.

Inside were rows of shops. Fabric shops, Asian groceries, cheap clothes. And a CD and DVD stall.

"Here is the best, most authentic pho in Berlin," Van said as we strolled down the dividing corridor. At the end was a restaurant with white-lace doily tablecloths. A young woman was unstacking chairs as we came over.

"Chao chi," Van called out and Truong nodded at her. She smiled and flashed five fingers at us. Then she brought over menus and tea for us to drink.

As always, I felt awkward, being served when I was used to doing the serving.

"What do you recommend?" I asked Truong.

"Đặc biệt," he said. Special.

When he ordered for us, I heard the Northern accent in his Vietnamese, chopping.

The taste of the tea brought me back to my usual reality. I glanced at Truong and he smiled, reminding me of the night we shared. Yes, he was still good-looking, and, even better, was still interested in me.

The pho was fresh, without MSG and, to me, bland.

"Your restaurant do it sweeter, with chemicals," he said, echoing my thoughts.

"You have to take us to your restaurant," Michael suggested. "We are connoisseurs of pho."

I liked how all his friends stuck to using German and didn't exclude Toby. I liked how he told the waitress that I was his girlfriend. I liked how his body was surrounded by a dragon.

I like him, I admitted to myself.

The pho was good and subtle without MSG. I could taste the aniseed and cinnamon and the Vietnamese mint was like lightning.

Almost as good as pho in Việt Nam.

"Have you been back to Việt Nam?" he asked.

"A couple of times. I'm going again in a few weeks with my mother."

"To Hanoi?"

"Yes. Our relatives are there."

When Truong held my hand, I felt buoyed up by his attention. He was happy and exhilarated and I felt so too, doubly so. When he directed his attention to his best friends their good regard made me feel more comfortable than I deserved.

And when we got up to go I felt his arousal hard and eager and my own desire delirious and dizzy. Everyone seemed to be super-sensitive and their smiles cut like knives. Truong and I walked ahead of the group and no one seemed to mind when we took the first taxi away from the hangars together.

When he kissed me, I felt a surge inside like a tsunami. The empathy drug I had taken was better than ecstasy. I felt my desire and his entwined, I was fucking and being fucked all at the same time.

Whatever it was, I wanted more of it.

And the means of getting it was through Truong.

HANOI – VUONG

I went back to my apartment where Camille was waiting. I didn't know what I was going to tell her. The Department wanted me to keep my visit to Lien secret. They didn't want the media to know that Lien was we. And always they threatened I could be pulled into the Department. I was allowed to live on the outside because I was good. Even Camille did not know that I was we.

Camille knew something was wrong as soon as our eyes met. She let me in the front door and closed it.

"What happened at work today?" she asked.

"I had a disturbing client," I said. If it was work Camille only got a few details, no identifiers and only part of the story. Confidentiality was part of my work. "She murdered her father because he killed a pet pig of hers."

"Oh, I remember reading about that one," Camille replied.

She folded me in her arms, but all I could feel was the sensation of we.

"You need something to distract you," she said.

Guiltily I paid attention to her. I flicked back her blonde hair and focused on her startling blue eyes – the most remarkable eyes I had ever seen.

"How was your day?" I said, remiss.

"Average. Some progress." Camille was a junior researcher for the Department in a different section. Her daily reports were shorter than mine. She went into the bathroom, her movements like the dancer she once had been.

"I missed you today," Camille said coming out of the bathroom with one hand closed. She sidled up to me on the couch.

"Is this a special occasion?" I asked.

"Every day is a special occasion," Camille replied, a twinkle in her eye. I held out my hand and she deposited a pink pill in my palm. Empathy. The female Viagra, they called it. It worked on the mind rather than the body.

I swallowed the pill dry. I could not refuse Camille anything, she was always there for me, my reality, unlike the memories of we. And empathy would take my mind off what happened today.

We sat next to each other on the bed, holding hands.

"The murderer. She was one of those multiples they found years ago, wasn't she?"

I could not reply. I wanted to say I was a multiple.

"Don't worry if you can't talk about it," Camille said and her finger stroked my cheek. The soft sensation doubled as the empathy took effect. I felt her concern like a warm blanket, and our mutual attraction pulling us to touch one another.

"Let me distract you," she said and put her hand between my legs. As we undressed each other I felt the slither of our desire and the headache manifesting between my brows faded away.

We curled up in each other's arms and I enjoyed the sleepy sensation and relaxation of our bodies. The residue of the empathy still made me shiver as she ran her finger up my arm. Post-sex with empathy was the closest I felt to being we away from my multiples. Involuntarily I flashed on Lien's dark eyes and the sure fit of her hands in mine.

"We are we," I murmured to myself.

"You and I are we," Camille replied, and I stopped myself from correcting her just in time.

Camille was not we. She was too individual. She sculpted in her spare time and I needed her to be different. She had a different perspective than we, and I sorely needed that.

I pulled myself up in my own thoughts. We were thinking like we.

Evelyn and the monitor were not in my thoughts. I didn't have to say "I" if we didn't want to.

"You're distracted again," Camille whispered in my ear and tickled me.

I felt the doubling of pleasure and squirmed happily in her grasp.

The next morning the computer chimed urgently, the special pitch reserved for Departmental communications. Swallowing my noodles, I went over to my screenpad. A message from Evelyn. I was being called in early for my check-up.

"Work," I said.

On the way into the Department I wondered what Camille would think if I told her I was a multiple. It wouldn't matter, I concluded. Camille loved me. We had been together for seven months and she had said it first, leaving me speechless. I had had a sense of déjà vu when we first met, she seemed familiar and our relationship had a synchronicity to it, we fell into each other's rhythms naturally. It was the easiest-forming relationship I had ever had – almost too good to be true. She had asked me out first too.

I would tell her tonight and be damned to the Department. There was too much I wanted to share with her now, and I didn't want to be distant from her. We could be we, I thought to myself.

Seriousness settled into my spine as the squat, grey, square building came into view. Even though I was staff now and not just a client, the Department intimidated me. The early conditioning they gave we was too strong.

As I swiped my pass the guard at the gate raised his eyebrows.

"You're cleared to go to Level 5 today," he said.

A cold ball formed in my stomach. The elevators only went to Level 4, though the building had six floors. It was a running joke that they did interrogations on the higher levels. At least, we thought it was a joke.

As I waited for the lift I ran over my conversation with Lien again. I hadn't done anything wrong, I told myself. As the lift bell chimed and I swiped my card I felt guilty anyway. I had become a little girl again, forced to become "I" and separated from "we."

When the lift door opened Evelyn was waiting for me on the other side.

"Hello, Vuong. We have some news for you."

"Good or bad?" The words escaped my mouth from nervousness as we walked down the corridor. The grey corridors looked the same as every other part of the Department that I'd been in.

"Both." Evelyn stopped in front of a closed door. She knocked and an older man opened it. His hair was black but speckled silver, unusual. Most would have had it dyed.

"Vuong. Evelyn." He nodded at the soft chairs in front of his desk.

"We are doing a check-up with you today, Vuong. To clear you to visit... Geraldine. She is a multiple as well. She lives in Australia. Her foster family gave her an English name."

Australia! I curbed the absurd gratitude I felt at being allowed to see another multiple.

"The bad news is Geraldine has stage-four cancer. She's dying."

Anger surged through me. They had waited this long to tell we that one of us was dying...

"She has requested to see the multiples, and at this stage only you can go. Accompanied by Evelyn, of course."

"What about the others?" I asked.

"You may see them if the visit goes well. Two others are also overseas. We kept you separated until you were mature enough to identify as 'I,' not 'we.'"

What was so magical about being twenty-five? I wanted to scream at them. Or burst into tears. We had been told that we had to be apart and that we would never see each other again.

"You know from your training that the brain is not fully mature until your mid-twenties," Evelyn said gently, recalling me to myself. She put her hand on my shoulder and involuntarily I felt the sympathy she was feeling for me. An after-effect of the empathy was being super-sensitive for a day or two later. I hated it at that moment. I would have preferred to dislike my monitor. Instead I understood her feelings and liked her more for it.

"We wanted you all to have the chance to individuate. I know culturally it is a matter of some contention among our international colleagues as to how appropriate it is, but the Department did not want your successful cloning to be known. And we couldn't keep you in an isolation ward forever, could we?"

His appeal to my sensibilities made me sick to the stomach. The absolute power they had over we was still evident. They controlled the media, and all access to their way. Most people did.

I remembered when cloning was touched on briefly during my university days. Prone to mutation and genetic failure. Was cancer just that, a genetic mutation? Everyone wanted to have a clone – it was a popular movie topic like having babies. But the risk of failing outweighed success.

I had once asked Evelyn who had cloned we. She had said it was Ma, working illegally, not able to have babies so she created we. I asked if we were clones of Ma and she said no. They had taken DNA samples from us and could not identify which was the original – if there was one. Evelyn speculated that we were born like identical twins from the same zygote. She did not tell me whether the others of we were flawed or not.

"Enjoy your contact with Geraldine. My condolences." Even without empathy I would have spotted the insincerity of his words. He did not know how to relate to women, let alone we.

"We're leaving this afternoon," Evelyn told me. "You may wish to tell Camille."

I flinched at the reminder that I was still under scrutiny. Then I followed her out the door.

I had lunch with Camille. I asked her to meet me at our favourite hawkers' corner. Beneath the concrete overpass old women made food for passers-by like they had for decades. Camille stood out in this part of Hanoi, and usually I would buy meals for both of us so we wouldn't get ripped off.

Seeing Camille in silhouette talking to our favourite pho vendor with her basic Vietnamese made things better all on its own. I wondered what I was going to say to her. That the multiples were still alive and with us was embargoed. I wanted to tell Camille but part of me shied away from the truth. How would she react knowing there were five of me scattered around the globe? The others were in Australia and New Zealand. Far enough away and quiet enough. America would have made it too political, or so Evelyn explained it to me.

I'm still special, I thought to myself. I wasn't dying, nor had I killed.

I was just another researcher with a psychology degree.

"Camille." I touched her on the shoulder. Camille smiled at me and all my fears sloughed away. She still loved me.

"Pho?" Camille asked.

"Chicken." The steaming-hot bowls of noodles were brought to us as we squatted on tiny plastic stools to eat. Not only was the food better, but it came at half the price than at a restaurant. Plus no one would monitor conversations under the overpass.

After our firt bites of pho I took my courage in my hands and spoke to Camille.

"I've been informed by the Department that I am a clone. The woman I saw who murdered her father is another clone of me." Camille's eyes widened, surprised. Then she put down her pho and gave me a hug. Her gesture almost brought me to tears.

"They're sending me overseas. To meet with the surviving multiples. They want an array to see if there are behavioural similarities." I told her half the truth. I kept to myself the games I used to play in front of the mirror.

"They are still alive?" Camille exclaimed.

"Yes."

"They are sending you by yourself?"

"No. With Evelyn. Another staffer."

"I'd like to see Australia," Camille commented. "When are you going?"

"This evening. This multiple is…" I choked on the words. "Dying. Of cancer."

Camille frowned. "I hope you can make it easier for her." Camille seemed to become distant then, it was disturbing her as much as me. "So you might get cancer too," she said, crystallising my fear.

"There's nothing I can do about it," I muttered, swallowing my pho noodles.

"You could die in a moped crash," Camille suggested.

"More probably," I replied.

"I'd like to meet the other clones. Do you think they'll let me?" Camille asked.

"I don't know," I said. "I'd like you to meet them too. See if they resemble me. I'm too close to it, literally."

"Well, you aren't a murderer," Camille confirmed.

"I don't feel empathy towards animals. I love eating meat too much," I confessed.

We sat on our plastic chairs, shoulders touching as we ate our pho.

"I still love you. If there are more benign versions of you out there that can only be a good thing," Camille suggested and squeezed my hand.

I was overwhelmed by her compassion. Even the idea of Lien did not faze her.

I appreciated Camille so much in that moment.

There was not much left to say.

The next morning, I awoke in a tangled buzz. I was sweaty and a mess but it did not matter. I slowly became aware of my surroundings. I was on a black couch at Truong's flat, I surmised. There were stacks of CDs and CD covers scattered in piles around the room.

A faint hangover lingered but was swept away when I saw him watching me waking up.

"How do you feel?" he asked with a throat full of smoke.

I smiled back as if drawn by a string of content. He shared my feeling and our skin tingled in a way that I had never felt with anyone before.

Was it hormones? Chemicals? Love?

"It's good, isn't it?" he said, making it clear what he put it down to.

"Yes," I said, with a tinge of disappointment that I couldn't hide.

"Empathy. It enhances what is already there," he continued.

I broke out into a smile again. I was like a teenager, an emotional virgin, this morning. I wanted to hold him, I wanted him inside me once more.

As if he could read my mind he embraced me and lingered over a long-drawn-out kiss.

It seemed so natural, the dance of the aftermath, what steps to take next. He was not in a hurry and neither was I. I wanted to find out his source of empathy and where I could get some. And pragmatically I wanted to find out when the inevitable crash would be.

"Your first time?" he asked, a few moments later.

"Yes. It's marvellous. Thank you for showing me."

"You're welcome. Next time you can bring some friends."

I blinked for a second. Did he mean he wanted group sex?

"Your friends can meet my friends and we can share empathy together. Not as a group if you're not comfortable with that. We can just use it like ecstasy and dance together. Maybe at Drei. Will you be going?"

I nodded. Drei was the marathon three-day dance party coming up in a month. For him to commit to meet up then spoke of a future...

I digested this and thought of Freja. She had had group sex before and she would enjoy a tryst with Truong. I felt unease. She would love empathy.

"When does the crash come?" I asked him. It was good, too good.

"It doesn't. You feel good and well inclined towards everyone. It tapers off after a while."

Somehow his explanation did not satisfy me. It was too easy.

"Really?"

"Really. It's pure, not cut with anything else. We source it straight from Việt Nam. No in-betweens."

I blinked at his revelation. From Hanoi to Berlin. It was not so far-fetched. But in Việt Nam recreational drug-dealing could lead to the death penalty. And no drug that could make you feel so good came without consequences. Humans were not built to be on a continual high.

I caught Truong smiling as he looked at me side-on. As if he could read my mind.

"It's all above-board in Việt Nam. It's mass-produced in labs like generic medicines. Because it hasn't been passed by bodies like the TGA in Western countries it is black-marketed and only used recreationally."

"Can you overdose on empathy?" There had to be a bad side. Side effects. Otherwise it was a party drug to replace all party drugs. A genuine aphrodisiac that made you feel how other people felt, an orgasm upon an orgasm.

"I don't think so. I've heard anecdotes of people being addicted to it, like sex addicts becoming more so. If you can be addicted to sex. I'm not sure you can be."

I was mute at that. I could easily fall for feeling that acute bolt of pleasure again and again. And I had a strong feeling that Truong was not telling the truth. But even this was eclipsed by my rising hunger.

We kissed again, long and drawn-out, and I was seized by a desire for him to penetrate me again, a desire I had only felt before in dreams. When he did so, just the skin-to-skin contact made me pulse with pleasure, wave after wave. Maybe this was what a vaginal orgasm was, something I had read about in magazines but I had never felt before.

This time I reluctantly broke off contact. I was so dizzy I wanted to feel grounded again. Soaring inside my own body I held his hand and the sensations doubled with my breath.

"I could do this all morning," I managed to say. Truong laughed gently.

"If only we had all morning. I'm expecting visitors at ten. You can stay but you may want to be dressed and showered by then."

I shook my head. "I'll go home." I pulled on my clothes and so did he, covering the eyes of the dragon on his chest. "So when shall I see you again?" The words and desire slipped out of my mouth before I could censure them. Suddenly I desperately needed confirmation that I could feel this way again.

"Tonight? I will drop around your restaurant."

I nodded, reassured. I stank in my sweaty clothes but from our mutual embrace it seemed he did not mind. The echo of our physical love tingled in my lips.

He walked me to the door of his flat.

"Sayonara, sister," he said.

"Adieu to you," I replied. The door closed behind me as I walked away and I felt a little pang at leaving.

I was feeling lovelorn-lost.

Ridiculous just after the one night, but that empathy was killer stuff. I tucked my hands into the sleeves of my wind-cheater as the cold winter air brushed past my warmed cheeks. The streets were empty in the early-morning light, and the apartments on the streetfront had their blinds and curtains closed against the cold.

Catching the U-Bahn back to Kreuzberg I reflected on the night, teasing myself with the sensory memories. My fingertips tingled on the edges of tracing the dragon tattoo on his chest. It was the empathy that made me super-sensitive as I felt the ridges of the scales and the flicker of the tongue of the dragon that embraced me. A flood of images enveloped me, the dragon plunging into me, winding around my body and Truong's.

My eyes snapped wide open as I almost missed my stop. Bolting out the door just in time, the cold hit me with physical force. I walked hurriedly down the concrete subway tunnel to emerge opposite the discount supermarket on the way home.

I brushed past an old woman bent over a shopping trolley and my breath stopped.

I was bowled over by layers of memory, like piles of mildewed old newspaper sinking into mould. Every step was a struggle in winter and hurt was in every movement.

I stumbled with the force of the feeling. Standing up straight, I turned to look at the retreating back of the old woman, shrouded in blankets.

I bit my lip and my own feelings returned, faintly reminiscent of Truong.

Shaking my head, I carefully continued walking home. So empathy worked by touch. Anyone I touched. I wondered how long it would last, and regretted I had not asked Truong.

Maybe this was what he was hiding…

I could text him a query.

I did so and sent it as I stumbled home.

The pavement was slippery with the remains of rain.

I approached the shower with trepidation and tentatively soaped my arms first. A warm feeling suffused me, and I was at home in my body again. I felt comfortable in the warm water with the relaxed lethargy I usually felt after sex. Eased, I put on fresh clothes and checked my phone.

Truong had replied: *It lasts as long as you want it to.*

Being deliberately obtuse, I thought.

The unwelcome suspicion came: how many girls had he given empathy to and shared this experience with? Had they all been craving it afterwards like I did?

Or, like dealing in other drugs, did they in turn pass it on to other lovers? Would I?

I was strictly a user of party drugs, not a supplier. I could not be bothered with the logistics or danger and didn't ordinarily need money that badly.

Could I have the experience I had with Truong with other people?

How about other women?

I was scared and excited, I admitted to myself.

How much would Truong ask for it? Would he supply me with it for money or would he want more for the same?

I floundered in my predictions of what I knew of him after one night.

In the kitchen I brushed past my mother and felt years of exhaustion at once. She was barely putting one foot in front of another.

This was what it was like to be my mother. I wanted to cry then and take her in my arms.

"Ma, are you all right? Sit down. I'll make you some tea," I said to her.

"No, daughter. I need to lie down," my mother said and suddenly I saw her true age and the depth of the lines of her face. She had always said that you could tell the true age of Asian women by the look of their hands, and today her hands were wrinkled like chicken feet.

She shuffled off to her bedroom and I retreated to mine, finally feeling the inevitable crash of post-party fatigue coming down.

I woke up and felt like a hollow shell. The vividness of my memory of the past twenty-four hours was bleached away. My senses were dulled. I missed the bright colours of my experience of empathy. I wanted more of it.

I had to see Truong.

I did not stop to think whether it was him I was missing, or the drug, or both.

I played Massive Attack as I got dressed, and found myself humming and dancing to it. I went into the kitchen where my mother was making a meal, her breakfast, my dinner.

I remembered feeling her age and sat down next to her at the kitchen table as she ate.

"How are you?" I asked.

She looked surprised, and I felt guilty for my benign neglect.

"I'm fine. I'm still alive," she replied curtly. "You have been out late again."

"Yes," I said. I wanted to tell her something, but what? I could not bring up Truong, not yet. She had only met one of my boyfriends and I couldn't call Truong that.

"You have been out with Freja," my mother said. "She is a fun girl."

I nodded. I thought she approved of Freja, but sometimes I wondered.

"How is work?" I asked and again I saw her surprise that I would ask.

"It is there," she said. "Why these questions?"

"I was just wondering how you are, Ma. We don't talk much and I was wondering…" If you were happy. I bit down on the words. It seemed too cruel a question. All she had was her work and her hui circle. They met weekly, a Vietnamese custom where each hui member deposited money in a pot. Members bid for the sum total for the week. After you won a bid you would then have to pay it back by putting money in the pot for the rest of the members to take turns winning the pot. It was a social occasion that involved dinner and gossip. My mother's hui circle dated back to when she had first migrated from Việt Nam to East Berlin to find work.

"How is the restaurant?" she quizzed me.

"It is there," I said.

I held her hand for a moment. I felt nothing, no echo of empathy.

I missed the drug, I concluded. I wanted to feel what my mother was feeling now.

"Have you met any boys?" she asked.

I hesitated for a moment. Then I took the plunge.

"Yes, I have. His name is Truong."

"North or South?"

I blinked. My mother still had hang-ups from the old days back in Việt Nam, when it mattered.

"His parents are Northern," I guessed from his accent.

"When am I going to meet him?"

"Soon," I said.

"What does he do for work?"

"He does music recording," I told her.

"So long as he makes you happy," she commented and I blinked back sudden tears. I was tired and emotional, so I thought. My mother could still surprise me. I thought she would be old-fashioned and conservative in her expectations of me and by extension whom I dated.

But my happiness mattered to her.

Impulsively, I gave her a hug. She resisted at first, then relaxed in my embrace.

"Cam on con," she said. Thank you, little one.

And I felt her immense gratitude, which made me feel even smaller inside.

Freja came by the restaurant as I was working in the early afternoon.

I held my breath waiting for my senses to pick up her emotions but the empathy appeared to have worn off. I was both relieved and disappointed when I could not read any more details as she bounced in, shiny from her last sexual encounter.

But she could read me.

"You picked up! I can tell by your inner glow!" I blushed, to her amusement. "My man was awesome. How was yours?"

I looked away.

"The best I ever had," I mumbled. My experiences were not as broad or as plentiful as hers.

As if on cue, Truong came through the doorway. He met my eye and I could not help but smile. He was eager to see me again. It had been less than twelve hours.

"Truong," he introduced himself to Freja.

"Freja," she said as she shook his hand, and she seemed to buzz full of energy to my tired eyes.

Maybe this was the comedown.

"So. We're going to Skoda to dance later. You coming?"

"Sure," I said.

"You too," Freja said to include Truong, who waited for my reply.

"Yes," I said. "Unless you've got other plans?"

"No." Truong grinned and my spirits lifted. He put his arm around me and suddenly everything seemed all right, like a familiar cliché.

I was super-aware of his shoulder touching mine. My desire threaded through my consciousness and I wanted us to leave so I could touch him again. I worked the rest of my lunch shift in a hurry, anticipating the fun time I was going to have with empathy.

I was pleased that Freja and Truong got to talking while I worked. I could feel Freja's approval in her ready smile and Truong was open to meeting people that mattered to me. He wasn't just after one thing and I appreciated that.

"Let's get a drink," Truong suggested as I knocked off from work.

We stepped outside the restaurant and I noticed a line of police cars parked illegally across the road.

"What's going on?" Freja wondered as we headed towards Alexanderplatz. The iconic radio tower loomed up above a milling crowd of people.

"There's a pro-immigration march today," Truong said.

"Oh yeah. I'd forgotten about that. I was going to go…"

But I forgot because of Truong.

"We can join in… They're expecting trouble though," Truong said.

"Damned neo-Nazis," Freja commented.

As we approached the public square people were milling around holding placards. We were in the pro-immigration part of the demonstration and were soon surrounded by masses of friendly people.

"Wilkommen!"

Welcome to all. It was a mixed crowd of Germans and visible foreigners. Supporters of immigration smiled at me, Truong and Freja. The streets became packed as people filled the square. Then the crowd noise increased to a chant. I saw a line of police up ahead with riot shields.

"Keine Nazis!"

Truong put his arm protectively around me. Freja stopped walking and so did I.

Up ahead a single line of police in riot gear ran interference between mobs of shiny white skinheads and protestors.

The flow of the crowd brought us close to the police. The protestors were pushing back against the neo-Nazis, who were surging against the police.

"No place for Chinese!" A skinhead spat in our direction over the shoulder of a policeman. The policeman pushed him back.

I recoiled from his hatred. It was not the first time I had been verbally abused, but it was the first time I felt concern for my actual safety.

"We should go," Truong said in my ear.

"We can't let them bully us into leaving. We have the right to be here like everybody else," I protested, swallowing my fear.

"It's getting ugly," Freja said. "I don't want to be around when the fighting starts. Let's go, My."

Reluctantly I let Freja and Truong lead us away from the action. I felt cowardly about my relief. I couldn't stand up for my principles. This was how the Nazis had won power.

But Freja was right. As we retreated I heard the crunch of a baton hitting flesh.

The demonstration dissolved into a melee of fighting and fleeing, of protestors trying to get out of the way of the police action.

In the news that night, the riot earned a brief mention of one hundred neo-Nazi arrests from a crowd of thousands.

Berlin had shown its ugly violent side again.

Sydney – Vuong

From the plane Australia was dry, brown and empty. My guidebook showed pictures of the cities, without the layers of flats that I was accustomed to seeing. The people on the plane were a mix of Asian and Caucasian. The Australians among them spoke accented English – even those that looked Asian.

After landing at Sydney Airport we took a train to Central, to board another train to the beachside, where Geraldine lived.

The air was sharp with the smell of eucalyptus when I disembarked, carrying my suitcase. Evelyn was not awed by the air or the emptiness, so I tried to emulate her, taking the spaces in my stride.

Evelyn hailed a taxi. On the trip to the hospice I marvelled at the large houses and units as we went past. They must still have large families in Australia, I thought.

Perhaps this rich democratic nation could afford it.

We stopped in front of an old colonial house.

Outside the air was spiked with salt and the chill of autumn.

We walked up the path to the front door, which swung open at Evelyn's footsteps.

A nurse greeted us.

"You must be here to see Geraldine. She'd be glad to see her sister." She clicked her tongue at me and showed us upstairs to the first floor. I found her English difficult to understand – the accent was elongated, unlike the American English I had learnt at school.

"First you need to wear a mask and sanitise your hands," she said, taking us to a nurses' station.

"Geraldine has a compromised immune system so we can't take chances with the different flu viruses around," she explained, almost apologetically.

I took the disposable blue mask I was given and rubbed the hand sanitiser in my hands. The scent reminded me of hospital bathrooms.

"She's in the sitting room."

We ventured into a large room with windows looking out onto the beach. Two residents were asleep in their chairs. Another was reading a book and looked up sharply when we walked past.

Geraldine was beside the window looking out. She must have heard us approach, for she turned around. Her eyes widened in recognition of me, and I smiled. In person she radiated an energy not evident in her photo.

Then she turned to Evelyn.

"I was told we were not going to be monitored," Geraldine snapped. Her vowels were broad and Australian. I could barely understand her English, but her intent was crystal-clear.

Evelyn, taken aback by her directness, could only nod.

"Call me when you're done," she said to me crisply and left me with Geraldine.

Geraldine did not stand up. She remained sitting, her legs covered by a blanket.

Up close I could see she was emaciated by chemotherapy, her cheekbones gaunt and her face hollow.

Yet she held her hands out to me and I took them.

I was drawn to place my cheek next to hers and felt a faint jolt, an echo of what I had felt with Lien. Again, I was moved to cry. But when I saw Geraldine's eyes, they were dry and sharp with anger.

"Bloody Department. We should have never been separated."

Involuntarily, I looked for the cameras in the room. The rest of the residents were ignoring us.

"Sit down. They don't monitor the likes of we. And you can talk openly here. They'd think you're kidding if we say you're a multiple."

Underlining the words was a savage humour. The experience of cancer had stripped back more than the flesh of her bones.

I obeyed her, sitting on a cane chair with a padded blue cushion. My suitcase sat next to me.

"I'm dying, Vuong, and I don't have time for politeness. You must excuse that. Have you had any problems?"

"No," I replied.

Except for the dreams.

I looked out the window at the grey ocean view. Geraldine was still holding my hands, her fingers wrinkled and dry.

"Ma should have never created us. I'm told I'm the first one to go. Bloody cloning. How are the others? They have not told me anything."

"I've only seen one. Lien. She murdered her foster father," I said through a dry mouth.

"Oh. So we go psycho too. Great. Only my body has let me down. Should be grateful for that I suppose." The bitterness surprised me. But I found her anger echoing in my body, tensing my muscles. "So why have you suddenly been granted access to we?"

I shrugged, not wanting to meet her eyes. My caution from years of monitoring could not be shed in a moment. "I'm a researcher," I admitted reluctantly. "They are worried that we become mentally ill, I suppose."

"I know what you do. Did the Department choose that for you?" I nodded. "Jesus. I can't imagine living the life you live. I cursed them when they sent me out of the country, but it was the only good thing they did for me. This is a fucking racist country though. They don't care about multiples, but if you aren't white…"

I nodded again, helpless in the face of her anger.

"Go get some tea for yourself," she suddenly ordered, briskly letting go of my hands.

Surprised, I got up. It was only out of the corner of my eye that I saw her wipe her eyes with her fingers.

I encountered the nurse on the stairs, who offered to get some tea for us.

"You're so pretty," the nurse said to me. "It makes me sad to see what Geraldine used to look like before the treatments. You're one lucky duck." She patted me on the arm as I went back into the sitting room.

When I sat back next to her, Geraldine took my hand again.

"You have to see the others. Give we my regards. I'd do it myself but I'm too weak. And we should go public. Tell the world what it's like to be multiple. So they stop cloning humans."

"It's illegal where I come…"

"It's possible. It won't remain illegal for very long." I knew what a Departmental creche would be run like and I shuddered. "You should tell the press," Geraldine pushed me.

"I can't. They'll discriminate against me or kill me." My fear came out in my words. "If Lien is outed as a multiple, they will ban cloning. But she would not survive long in rehabilitation."

"Damn," Geraldine fumed, her hand clenching and unclenching around mine. Her grip was as sharp as a bird's claws, but I hid my discomfort.

"We have to do something. You can recommend that we reunite, can't you? I want to see we before I die."

"I can try," I said weakly. "I want to see we too."

Her eyes softened at my admission. Her hands relaxed.

"I've never been to Việt Nam. Do you like it there?"

"I don't know anything else," I said. "Australia seems nice, but it's empty." Lonely, I thought. At home this sitting room would be full of people talking.

"Did you ever see Ma again? I wonder what happened to her. I tried looking it up in the press and it mentioned she was in rehab."

"I don't know." It shamed me suddenly that I had not sought out Ma myself as an adult. I knew why – we had been told by the Department not to look for Ma. But I still could have tried when I was unmonitored. "Ma loved we. Wanted we. She used to sing songs to we. Do you remember?"

Geraldine's eyes softened. "Cat's in the cradle with the silver spoon," she sang. "She would be a talented scientist. Wasted in rehab. I wonder whether they used her in research. It might be why we can't find out anything about her. I wonder whether they made her create anymore multiples."

"There's only we," I protested weakly.

Geraldine snorted.

"Are you the original?" she asked.

"I don't know," I said honestly. "Does it matter?"

"I guess it doesn't. But don't you want to know if you'll end up like me? Or Lien?"

I won't end up like either of you, I thought defiantly, but I didn't say it.

"We should not have been created. I wonder what Ma had in store for us."

The thought sent a chill down my spine.

"Maybe she just wanted five children," I suggested.

Geraldine laughed harshly. "Ma was old. And rich. She would have paid for surrogate mothers to have we. Maybe the original is still around outside of Departmental control. Maybe we will meet her one day."

I chewed on my lip. I did not like the picture that Geraldine was painting. I had clung to the utopia of our childhood. We were all special. Ma had told us so.

"If I met Ma, I'd slap her. Do you reckon the Department would let you meet her if you asked?"

"I already tried," I said softly. In my adolescence I had demanded to see my real mother and was refused. They were punishing Ma by never allowing her to see we again.

But we were being punished too – for being born.

"Do you think we look like Ma?" Geraldine asked. I shook my head. Geraldine sighed. "I wondered if we were related to her at all. In my worst nightmares I dream that Ma had cooked us up to use our organs for the original."

"She wouldn't have done that," I retorted too quickly. We were special. Ma loved we. "The Department wouldn't dare create more multiples. They don't know if we will survive for very long…" I bit my tongue. "They don't want killers like Lien around."

"They realise that now," Geraldine said. "But you can't think that the Department is very long-sighted. If some-one in the government wanted a multiple, they would have found a way. You have to find out what you can."

"I'm monitored," I reminded her.

"I have a desktop. I can try. I've been following genetic science but there's a lag between discoveries and their reporting. There was no sudden jump in knowledge after they took us away."

I swallowed. Compared to Geraldine I had exhibited no curiosity about our past. The conditioning of the Department was too strong. It was not until I was fifteen that I had my own desktop and my own room.

Maybe living in Australia made you more curious.

"Damn it that I'm dying! I wanted to see we for so long. Why couldn't they have let us see we when I was strong?"

Her hands clenched in mine again and I saw the same longing in her eyes that I had seen in Lien. It was reflected in me too.

"They are scared of we," I said.

Geraldine laughed, not unkindly.

"You may have something there, Vuong." She smiled. "We are going to find the others," she said before I could form the words.

"How come you never saw them?" I whispered to Geraldine.

"I wasn't allowed to. They didn't want us to meet up until we were individuated."

"You mean…"

"Until we were adult. So we wouldn't be we again. I guess now they don't care, now they know we can die young. They told me I would be taken to see them when I'm better. Now they say I'm too sick to travel, and they wouldn't let me overseas anyway, being so sick like this. I have been e-mailing them every day. They seem nice enough but it's not the same as meeting up with we..." Geraldine's eyes filled up with tears again. "I don't know why we in Aetearoa never came to visit me. I don't know what it is like over there. Be careful, won't you?"

She hugged me close and I felt a wall dissolve inside me again. It was like we were being hugged by Ma.

I could feel Geraldine wishing me well, and anger inside her like a fishhook. Frustration at being too sick, and angry we were apart. Part of her didn't want to see me only to be parted from me again, I realised.

Her rage was enough to kill, and I drew back. I looked into her eyes fearfully and saw her anger subside.

"I am so angry I could kill something," she said, echoing my thoughts.

Suddenly I remembered holding hands around the dinner table with Ma. We were thinking together and eating together at the same time. We would dissolve into play spontaneously and if one of us needed to go to the toilet we would all need to go.

I remembered what I felt with Lien.

What would happen if we all could get back together again?

Excitement kindled inside me. I could go over to New Zealand and get the others to come to Australia and there would be four of us. Then we would be we again.

Evelyn took me out to debrief.

I knew it was part of Evelyn's reporting to the Department, not because she wanted to ensure I was still healthy.

For someone who was going to die at twenty-five, Geraldine had spunk.

I did not want to die. Nor did I want to turn psychotic.

There was a desktop and I was tempted to call Camille. But I did not trust myself to be able to speak to her and not reveal what I was truly thinking and feeling.

What would be a healthy response to seeing a multiple on the brink of death?

I was sobered and scared.

Am I the original?

People made a big deal about being original, which I had not understood until now. If being the original meant that I was stronger and healthier than the others, then I wanted to be the original.

Was there more than one we?

When we were younger, we would pretend that we would meet another we. We knew from television that we were not supposed to exist – that multiples were the stuff of science fiction. We saw that multiples were evil on TV and we asked Ma about it. Ma laughed and said you could not believe everything you saw on TV. It made we wise.

Ma said that we were good girls and gave us treats.

We were special, she told we.

My debriefing with Evelyn took place on the ferry to the Opera House and under the Sydney Harbour Bridge. I began to suspect that she wanted me to know that she was not monitoring me as she should – that she was on our side.

Seagulls cawed in the air as I told her that Geraldine was dying and how much it scared me. I did not tell her about Geraldine's wanting to find Ma, nor of her urge to go public. The sea breeze was clean and fresh, free of pollution.

"It would be interesting," Evelyn said neutrally as the ferry moved into the harbour, "to know how culturally different you are. You had the same unique culture living in a creche and then she was brought up in Australia and you in Việt Nam. It would make an interesting study."

"Aren't you doing that already?" I asked and Evelyn looked at me side-on.

I realised that this was the first time that I had questioned Evelyn of my own accord. Geraldine's feistiness was infectious. I had become bolder myself. If Evelyn was my key to getting a reunion, then I wanted to sound her out before I trusted her.

Evelyn took a moment before replying.

"Of course we are. By observation. But if we wanted to interview you both we would need your consent."

I laughed out loud. "You did not ask for our consent when you carried out the biggest intervention of our lives!"

Evelyn had the grace to look ashamed.

"The Department is trying in its limited way to do the right thing by you. But we weigh up what is good for Việt Nam as well. We do not want a witch hunt of killing multiples."

"How can you release the research without telling people that we are still around?" I asked her.

"We wouldn't release the research into the public domain," Evelyn said. "We already have a vast amount of information that we are building on from studying you five."

Even though I knew about the regular monitoring and the tests I had to sit for the Department, for Evelyn to talk about the research so bluntly made me want to hit her.

"Am I going to get to see what you have discovered about we?" I enquired.

"We are judging that. You are the best qualified out of the multiples. But we have to decide if it is in your interest to know."

The ferry began disembarking. People around us were ignoring us.

"The more self-knowledge I have, the better off I will be," I said, trying to surf my rising anger. "Wouldn't you want to know if I was having homicidal thoughts like Lien? I could report that and you could put me in rehab…"

My voice was becoming shrill. A part of me was appalled. Somehow my veneer had cracked after seeing Geraldine. I could not play the part of the good multiple anymore.

I was too scared. They knew Geraldine was dying. Just suppose they knew that the rest of we would be dying too.

The Department could afford all the genetic tests it wanted.

"I'm trying to do my best," Evelyn said quietly to me. "I know it's hard on you. But even us monitors are not fully informed. We know we are reporting parts for a greater whole but only seniors know the whole picture."

We walked off the ferry into Circular Quay. An Aboriginal busker was playing a long cylindrical horn that made sounds like the calls of wildebeasts.

I choked back on my feelings. I had to play the good multiple to the hilt.

I was fooled into thinking that Evelyn was on the side of we. That the Department was consistent. That what happened to me was inevitable.

Jealousy warred with hatred and anger as Evelyn led me to a cafe and sat me down at a table. I wanted to walk away.

Taking a deep breath, I closed my eyes.

Exhaling, I pushed my emotions away, as I had thousands of times before.

Then I opened my eyes, my face a mask once more.

That night I was left alone in my vast hotel room. Jet lag pulled on me, but I couldn't sleep. Geraldine's face kept coming back to haunt me. She was dying and her last wishes were to see all of we.

The room had a desktop and I used it to pull up old news about we. It had been a long time since I had looked at the photos of us, five in a row dressed in rehab clothes, holding hands. I choked back on my tears as I read for the thousandth time how the little girls were going to be separated to lead normal lives.

How could they know what was best for we?

I clenched my fists and remembered the crinkly feel of Geraldine's skin.

We were dying.

I could die.

And the Department would not tell me.

The news did not tell me where the other two were. But I was a researcher.

To my surprise there were no restriction codes on the desktop.

Australia was a democracy, I reminded myself.

I had found we.

Two of we had been brought up together in Aotearoa.

I choked on my rage. Two of us had been left together! Why couldn't all of us stay together? I thought they had been separated like I had been separated from Lien!

I remembered night after night crying into my pillow in the orphanage because I was so lonely.

I looked at the clock. Four in the morning.

I had my own credit card and passport. Evelyn was asleep next door.

There were no cameras in the room.

Maybe they trusted me, I thought. Or perhaps in Australia monitors did not look after people 24/7.

I still could not relax. I wondered about Geraldine. What was her life like before she had cancer? She had shown me pictures of her family, a white family with brothers with blonde hair.

She had been a shop manager before she got sick. What she told me made me dizzy with the possibilities. Australia was not like Việt Nam. The government did not control people to the same degree. She had hidden that she was we too, though her foster parents knew.

She had monthly blood tests like I did and was monitored by fortnightly appointments. They had kept track of all of we that way, even overseas.

I wanted to tell Camille. I would when I got back. I sent her e-mails saying that we would talk about what I saw and that it was classified. She said she understood.

I missed her arms around me in the big bed. I missed what she would think about Geraldine and Lien. I needed her, now more than ever.

In the morning Evelyn greeted me in the breakfast room in the hotel. She was smiling, and it changed her face. She looked almost beautiful.

"We've been approved to see the other two multiples. And you won't be monitored. Instead we would like you to report on your visits with all four of them. Your observations and especially how you feel."

I swallowed my weak coffee and tried not to gag. I did not want the Department to know the extent of we. They might use it against we. To distract Evelyn, I asked her another question.

"Can we have a reunion? With all five of us? It might make Geraldine feel better before she dies…" I did not mean to plead like a little girl. But that was what it felt like.

"I'll ask," Evelyn replied.

Aotearoa was a four-hour plane trip from Sydney. They needed the ocean to keep us apart, I thought.

On the flight I reflected on what I would write for the Department. I did not want them to know how close we still were.

I could just write about my observations of the other multiples without writing much about myself.

I could write what they expected – I was accustomed to doing that and hiding my true feelings. The Department still had its grip on me, even when I was unmonitored.

I closed my eyes, hiding my tears from Evelyn, and pretended to nap.

Berlin – My

That evening as we waited for the U-Bahn on our way to Skoda, Truong produced the heart-shaped lollies again.

I eagerly swallowed them dry. I wanted to forget about the afternoon rally, and this was the best way.

"Freja?" he offered. She took one with raised eyebrows. "It's an aphrodisiac. Empathy."

"Sure," she said and swallowed.

We boarded the U-Bahn train and Freja's eyes seemed to sparkle under my scrutiny.

I put my arms around Truong, aroused and playful, and he smiled.

Then Freja brushed against him flirtatiously and he winked at her.

Truong held my hand and I was jolted back into his sensual world again.

Jealousy hit me then suddenly evaporated in desire for Freja. I wanted to kiss her.

Confused, I let go of Truong and stared at him and Freja.

Freja looked at me, then at Truong.

"This stuff is worse than ecstasy. I want to fuck everybody," Freja declared.

"Please don't," said Truong. "This dose is too pure. You're only supposed to feel a little bit." He held out his hands placatingly.

"Our stop." Freja bounced off the carriage, followed by Truong.

Seething with desire, I went after them. I could not stay angry at them. I was attracted to them both, and I didn't want to feel this way.

"Don't worry about it. It wears off."

I didn't know if Truong was talking to me or Freja.

"It's not all bad," Freja commented as we made our way down a back street.

Freja followed a map on her phone.

We came to an iron corrugated fence with a jagged hole cut in it and ducked in.

Freja led the way through the back door of the house into a dark club room filled with dry ice. Truong managed to slip his arm around me and I found myself in his embrace again. Reluctantly, I felt pleasure in his touch and the feeling wiped away my resentment.

A little voice inside my head whispered my doubt. How did I really feel about him? Would I spare him a second glance without the empathy?

Freja bounced back into my line of sight and encircled both of us in her arms. I felt a pulse of energy as she met my eye and smiled.

Whatever. I should just enjoy the trip, I decided, as Truong kissed me.

By the end of the night Truong had barely left my side but had made five sales of empathy. People knew who he was and where to seek him out. They were all friendly, some a little too friendly, bending in and pecking me on the cheek. I was so buzzed on happiness that my observations of their desire and desperation were of pity rather than scorn. After all, I had seen that gap when coming down off empathy and I had to be careful that I wasn't becoming a junkie too and a slave to empathy's desire.

"Thanks a million, Truong! Goodbye loneliness!" crowed a boy who did not look old enough to purchase alcohol.

It didn't bother Truong at all, he just kept by my side and danced with me. This time the buzz felt familiar, and I was content just coasting along. When I touched Truong, I felt satisfaction as well as a tinge of edginess. He was concerned about something and he was not caught in the moment of empathy like he had been the previous night.

"Your mother cleans for CHESS? That's interesting," Truong said. I took no notice of his comment at the time, I was too preoccupied surfing the waves of feelings I was receiving from empathy.

Truong was coasting on contentment, shaking hands and hugging everyone he came across. The good will seemed catchy, everyone was smiling and getting along. Empathy was truly a party drug. I did not even need to drink alcohol to relax anymore.

Freja introduced us to Mattias, a man she was seeing for the third time, which made him almost a regular. He shared empathy and his blue-eyed smile at me lifted my spirits disproportionally.

Tucked under Truong's arm, I was surprised when he asked about my mother again.

"Do you think you could get access to CHESS via your mother?" Truong asked.

I shrugged. I felt a tinge of tension in Truong. Something was wrong.

"CHESS is developing a drug that will supersede empathy. We would like to know more about it."

"Who is we?" I asked.

"My international hui group. We invested in empathy and we make a killing since we import directly from Vietnamese pharmaceutical companies. This new drug would either compete with us and wipe us out, or we could copy it and make a killing."

I blinked. The empathy told me he was telling the truth.

"I can ask my mother..." I said.

"She may not know what to look for," Truong said bluntly.

"She's not stupid," I retorted.

"You could cover one of her shifts, or accompany her?"

"I don't know..." I crossed my arms.

"We'll pay you. Cash and empathy. I won't ask you to do anything illegal. Just what you are comfortable with."

He wanted to appease me, and I let him embrace me. I needed the money and what he offered was six months' pay from the restaurant. All he wanted was a map of the inside of the factory.

If I asked my mother, she would want to know why. And she would not be sympathetic to a drug-run hui circle.

I thought of what I could do to get what Truong wanted. I had been to CHESS for my annual health check-up and the occasional doctor visit. My mother got free medical benefits for family as an employee.

When my mother was at her hui circle for the day, I would use her security pass and sneak into the factory wearing her uniform. It would be Sunday so not many people would be around. Us Asians looked much the same anyway.

Anything seemed possible with empathy.

It seemed so easy, a simple way of getting Truong what he wanted.

I rode on Truong's happiness with me and Freja's high with Mattias. Things were good then – never better.

I excused myself early that Saturday night and crashed at home at one that Sunday morning, coming off the empathy high. This time when I woke up to a dreary, cardboard-like mood I was prepared for it. I had a Red Bull with breakfast and the cobwebs were sliced away with the caffeine hit.

My mother said goodbye to me as I waited impatiently, and I felt an echo of edginess from her too.

I was too preoccupied to wonder why she was tense going to her hui circle.

I waited for five minutes then went into her room to get her uniform.

It was a tight fit and unattractive. I found her key pass in her drawers and tucked it into my pocket. Then I put on the hair net.

I found myself diminishing in the uniform. Unconsciously, my posture changed as I put on my sneakers. As I left the apartment, I felt like I had become invisible, another menial going to work.

The hustlers didn't bother to approach me at the U-Bahn station. I became alert as I got off at the stop for CHESS, but all was quiet. The factory compound was surrounded by tall wire fencing with a boom gate for entry. Next to the boom gate was a guard house and a door gate.

Taking a breath, I walked to the guard house. The guard, who was young, possibly younger than me, waved me through. I swiped the card on the pad and he did not even check the photo ID.

I approached the brown brick multi-storeyed building in front of me. Everything seemed closed for the weekend.

I swiped my way through the sliding doors of the front entrance to the reception desk in the slick, modern foyer.

On the wall I found a map of the floor with offices and labs and detailing fire exits.

I took a picture of it with my phone.

This is pretty easy, I thought.

Now to find the R and D labs.

I wandered down the corridor. I happened upon the cleaning closet, which also required a swipe in with ID.

Getting a vacuum cleaner to carry on my back was cumbersome but an essential prop, I thought.

Then I went down the corridor.

First there were doors to offices. They looked like standard offices to me – not of much interest.

Then I came upon doors leading to chemical labs.

I tried to swipe my way into them, but they wouldn't open.

Instead, I looked through the thin glass windows of the doors.

I went back up the corridor to the offices and swiped my way into one of them.

I found myself faced with locked filing cabinets and a messy desk with random papers piled on high.

Opening the desk drawers, I found a tablet foil – but it only contained aspirin.

I heard something and I quickly shut the drawer as a man entered the office. He was in a lab coat.

"Hello. Are you new here?" he asked.

"Yes," I said quickly.

"ID?"

I gave him my mother's ID, my stomach sinking.

His gaze widened and he gave the ID back.

"Apologies, I didn't realise it was you. You look different in the cleaning uniform."

"It's genius having you undercover here," he said. "No one would ever suspect you. We can't be too careful. Industry espionage being what it is."

Did he think I was my mother? Who did he think my mother was?

"You'd be pleased we have almost reached saturation point." He looked at me expectantly. Frozen, I nodded.

"You don't want to talk while undercover? You ex-Stasi are old-fashioned that way. I'll let you get back to your cover and cleaning."

He touched his forehead with a finger and left the office.

I stared after him, a thousand questions in my mind.

I started the vacuum cleaner so I could think.

My mother going undercover as a cleaner? What was she covering for? What was the "saturation point"?

It sounded crazy. Was I imagining things? Maybe the empathy withdrawal was making me hallucinate.

I wanted to run out of the factory and confront my mother, to see her everydayness and be comforted by her ordinary plainness. But first I had to finish the vacuum cleaning.

I vacuumed three offices and found nothing of worth. All this risk for no gain, I thought in frustration as I exited the building. Except the puzzle of my mother.

I went home and took off the uniform in relief. Back in my ordinary clothes of jeans and a T-shirt, I felt like myself again.

At the back of my mind I thought about empathy, but it was eclipsed by what I was going to ask my mother when she came home. How could I ask about what that man said without revealing the source? What did I want to know?

I knew that my mother's hui circle dated back to her arrival in Berlin, when it was full of Northern Vietnamese living in East Germany. They always helped each other out with finance when members needed it. They were my mother's only friends, or so I thought. But I did not know who they were. They could have contacts in the Vietnamese Communist Party...

I texted Truong and invited him over to our flat.

My mother came home. I made her a cup of tea.

"I have invited Truong, my new boyfriend, to meet you," I told her nervously.

She brightened up and I felt guilty for what I had done behind her back. I let her change and cook herself supper. She seemed to just be following her usual routine. Nothing seemed abnormal, and I hesitated about confronting her with the questions brought up by the man in CHESS.

Truong came by carrying flowers before I had a chance to ask her.

My mother smiled at him when he gave her the flowers.

"How did you meet my daughter?" she asked, sitting us down in the lounge.

"At the pho restaurant where she works," Truong replied.

"And you work in music," my mother confirmed, and to my relief Truong nodded. "And your parents? What do they do?"

"They have retired and gone back to Việt Nam," he said, and I was ashamed that I did not know and hadn't thought to ask.

"When did they come over?"

"In the late seventies."

"Same with me," my mother said. "I work as a cleaner for CHESS." Then her phone rang, a corny Vietnamese pop melody. "Excuse me," she said and went into the kitchen.

Me and Truong exchanged glances.

She was gone a long time.

"I've got to go," Truong said. "Apologies to your mother."

He gave me a peck on the cheek and left.

It seemed like forever before my mother joined me again for tea.

She glared at me and I swallowed nervously.

"That was a long call," I started.

"You know what this is about," my mother said. "You infiltrated CHESS using my uniform. What for? Was it for that boy?"

"Are you a spy?" I blurted out.

"This isn't about me. It's about you and what you did. You could get me into serious trouble." She had all but confirmed it with her avoidance.

"Do you work for the Vietnamese government?"

"Is Freja in on this too?"

"No, Freja doesn't know," I said. "Are you ex-Stasi?"

"I don't know what to do about you. What have you told your friends?"

"Nothing. I just got them a map of the factory," I admitted.

"That's industrial espionage, My. I said I would deal with you."

"Everything you told me was a lie..." I felt myself tearing up.

"I would have told you eventually. But you forced me to by your actions."

"Ma, you lied to me!"

"I'm sorry but I had to. You are too young to understand."

I tried to feel what she was feeling but the empathy had worn off. I could not tell if she was being sincere or not. I missed the certainty the drug gave me. It was too incredible, my mother the ex-Stasi. Everything she did not say was pointing to it.

"I was protecting you. I didn't want you to be tainted by the past. But now you've come to their attention. You need to know what you are endangering with your antics. You're old enough now." I stared at her in silence. She was confirming the conspiracy theory of the strange man in the factory. "We are trying to maintain peace in Berlin. The empathy drug pacifies people, and its popularity ensures a wide infiltration of people. We provide a good-quality product to maximise the effect. You know. You've tried it."

I goggled at her. She knew more about me and the black market than I knew myself through Truong. I felt an echo of the peace and happiness I had felt at Skoda. Instinctively, I knew she was telling truth.

So was Truong, from a different angle.

With the rise of the neo-Nazis I understood why drugging the population might appeal. But the comedown and possible side effects?

I still felt emptied and a shell of my usual self after empathy. Everyone wanting to make love could have unintended consequences, I could foresee.

"Have you tried empathy?" I asked my mother.

"No," she told me.

"How do you know that it is a good thing to do?" The audacity of the decision to affect the extensive club scene of Berlin staggered me.

"We have been observing for a long time. And most recently I've been watching you. You seem happier." I could not deny that. "My, you've almost compromised my position at CHESS. We are keeping an eye on their operations. I've been asked to get you to tell me about Truong and what he wants. I told them you were working for me to avoid further trouble. Please make this true."

I could not deny my mother anything. So I told her about Truong and what he knew of CHESS operations.

She just nodded. She seemed unsurprised by any of it.

"That was what we thought," she said, confirming my conclusions. "Thank you, daughter. Now, what I need you to do is go back to him as if nothing has happened. Just act normally. Tell me if he wants more. I'll take care of this."

I did not think I could live normally anymore. Not after my mother's revelations. She was so much more than I knew. My respect and admiration for her had increased exponentially.

Even though I was unsure about the wisdom of what her hui circle was doing, I had to catch up with Truong and tell him the truth.

But first I caught up with Freja. She appeared at the restaurant at the end of my shift. She was on edge. Immediately, I guessed she was on an empathy comedown.

"Will Truong come by soon?" she asked after giving me a hug.

"I expect so," I said. I hung up my tea towel and sat down. "I've had the most amazing couple of days," I began. "I found out my mother is spying on CHESS."

"No way," said Freja.

"Her hui circle is supplying the empathy black market with quality product from Việt Nam in order to pacify the population."

"That's crazy," said Freja.

"It's true. You've seen what empathy can do."

"No. It's crazy. Your mother, a spy and controlling people by empathy? That's crazy talk. You've taken too much empathy."

I opened my mouth to protest, then shut it again.

"It's true," I said. "I took her uniform and went into CHESS to map where the R and D labs were for Truong."

"You did what?"

"I went into CHESS and this man thought I was my mother and he talked about infiltrating the black market for empathy…"

"My, that's serious shit you're talking about. You wouldn't have done that. You're hallucinating."

I fell quiet. Everything I was saying was making things worse.

"Truong will verify what I've said," I declared. An awkward silence ensued. "How's Mattias?"

The diversion worked and Freja gave a long monologue of her love interest, interrupted only by Truong arriving.

He gave me a kiss and Freja a hug.

"Do you have any empathy on you?" Freja asked immediately.

Truong was taken aback but produced the heart-shaped pills. Freja swooped on them and swallowed them dry. I frowned. She was acting like a junkie.

And she was accusing me of being substance-affected…

I went to take one, but Freja put her hand on my arm.

"I don't know if My should take any more empathy. She's been having hallucinations and delusions," she told Truong.

"She has? That's not a usual side effect of empathy but there's always a first time. What has she been hallucinating about?"

"I am here, you know," I protested. They could ask me directly.

"Her mother being a spy. You wanting a map of CHESS."

Truong's eyes darted quickly from side to side.

"What are you talking about? That sounds paranoid," Truong said.

I wanted to hit him. But I had picked up on his body language. Perhaps it was not safe to talk in the restaurant. Maybe he didn't want Freja to know.

Boldly, I took the pill from him and swallowed it with a cup of lukewarm tea.

"I'm worried about you. Maybe I should take you home," Truong suggested.

"I'm fine," I said irritably as they shepherded me out of the restaurant.

"I have what you want on my phone," I said.

"What?" Truong asked.

"I'll show you. Both of you," I took out my phone and scrolled down the photo app.

There was a selfie of me and Truong at Berghain. One of me and Freja. Then nothing. Nothing from the last two days.

"I took a picture of the map," I protested. "When I went to CHESS. It should be here!" Mother. She must have deleted it when I was sleeping.

"That's delusional, My. You need to take some anti-psychotics," Freja suggested. She was the regular drug user, not me. She thought she knew what to do with someone out of her mind.

"And I know what I'm talking about," Freja continued.

I was speaking my thoughts out aloud again.

"I have anti-psychotics at home. We can go get them now. We don't want to worry your mother too much," Truong said.

"I don't want to go to…"

Truong and Freja frog-marched me to the U-Bahn, making it clear they would physically drag me to Truong's apartment if they had to. The empathy amplified their concern for me and swamped my protest. And to my surprise I felt tenderness from Truong. Something resembling love. I wallowed in it, forgetting for a moment my resistance to them both.

If this was the effect of empathy on people, surely it was a good thing?

But the side effects? If I was to entertain the thought for one second that the conspiracies I had discovered were not real…

I shied away from what that could mean for me and my sense of reality.

I breathed in and out and felt Truong and Freja's care and love for me amplified. I loved them back, even if they were wrong. And anti-psychotics couldn't hurt me, could they?

At Truong's apartment he presented me with an unmarked tablet foil.

"It's a generic anti-psychotic," he said. "Take two now, then one daily at night until the symptoms go away."

"I told my mother about you and the empathy black market. Her hui circle is interested in what your hui circle is doing," I blurted out.

"I doubt that very much," Truong said.

"They want peace in Berlin," I said. "Empathy is one way of achieving that."

"If only that were true," Truong replied. His dismissal cut me to the bone thanks to the empathy. But his concern rose again, and I could not stay mad at him. I began to realise what a mood-altering substance empathy was.

Then the anti-psychotic effects hit me, and my mood slumped to neutral-sedated.

"I feel weird," I complained.

"We'll take you home to bed," Freja said. "Sleep it off."

I knew they cared for me – I remembered that as they took me home.

I just didn't feel it anymore.

I didn't feel anything anymore.

Auckland – Vuong

Khanh and Giang lived in the suburbs of Aotearoa. Like Australia, it was spacious but green. They lived in a large apartment by Vietnamese standards.

As we went into the block of flats, a man walked past us.

"Hi, Giang," he said.

We strode up stairs that smelt of cat piss and knocked on the first brown door that presented itself.

"Coming," a woman's voice rang out and the accent grated on my ears. But it was definitely the voice of we.

When the door opened, we looked at us from behind glasses.

"I'm Khanh," said one, in a green jumper.

"I'm Giang. You are Vuong," said the other, in a red jumper. They smiled together and I could not help but grin back.

Their contentment radiated out from them, infecting me.

Giang embraced me. Khanh followed suit and infused me with a warmth and inclusion I had not felt for twenty years.

"We are glad to see you," Khanh nodded her head.

"Have you eaten?" Giang inquired and I nodded.

We sat back down on an apricot-coloured couch set. Their lounge room was lined with bookshelves with an eclectic mix of books, fiction and non-fiction, with psychology texts in particular.

I found myself disconcerted looking at them both after so many years and I felt their eyes on me, searching for reassurance.

"This is awkward," Giang said. "You look younger than your picture. Younger than us."

"It's my haircut," I said, embarrassed.

I wanted to embrace them again. But I sensed that they did not need to, that they had each other.

"We are sad about Geraldine and Lien." Giang bit her lip and I wanted to laugh aloud at the pleasure of recognising her mannerism. "We are afraid that something might be wrong with we too. So far the monitoring shows nothing but you do not know. We feel sorry for you three being alone. But you are not alone anymore!" Khanh clapped her hands in delight. "This is a special occasion. We'll have some champagne to celebrate. Then we will have some lunch, we cooked dim sum for you."

I grinned at them, and they happily went into the kitchen.

Champagne was poured.

"I do not drink normally. I go bright-red," I told them as Khanh filled my glass.

"So do we. But it does not matter at home, does it?" Giang said merrily.

We clinked glasses together and I tasted the champagne. It fizzed on my tongue and smelt faintly of burnt toast.

"You are a researcher." Khanh looked at me keenly. "So you would know if there was something wrong with we."

"I don't think there is anything wrong with we," I said bravely. "We were special. Then the Department split us up."

"Yes. I dreamt about that last night," Khanh said. "It was a nightmare." Giang nodded sympathetically. "Are you a monitor?"

"No. I only do research," I told them.

"Only. You do research, not only research. We're just secretaries. Of different departments but the same organisation. It keeps us in pennies."

Giang went into the kitchen to fetch the dim sum. I settled back on my soft-backed chair.

"This must be strange for you. Maybe it is not so strange for we. We want to see Geraldine and Lien too. But we didn't because…" She cut herself off.

"They should have left we in pairs," Khanh said, bringing out a plate of steamed dumplings.

"Someone would have been left alone," Giang corrected her.

"Not if there were more of us. How do we know there were only five? One of us could have been paired with the original."

I blinked. Giang and Khanh had assumed we were all clones.

"You think that there is an original out there that looks like we."

"Of course there is. We are all the same. We are multiples so there is bound to be something wrong with us genetically."

"We and the whole human race," I retorted. Geraldine's attitude was catching.

"Most humans are lonely," Giang said as Khanh served me a dumpling on a small plate. "They are not as lucky as we."

"You think we are lucky?" I said.

"We are lucky. Those of we that were forced to be alone are not so lucky. We hope to make it up to you somehow. We are sorry."

"It was the Department that separated us. You have nothing to be sorry for," I told them. "I think one of us is the original. It's not Geraldine. Probably not Lien. But one of us three."

Giang and Khanh looked at each other and I felt a distance opening between us.

"We are used to thinking as we," Giang explained as Khanh ate a dumpling. "We know that other people are used to being unique. They value being an individual. But we prefer to be the same. Other people find us disconcerting. But we notice that when people are in groups, they like being the same too. Like in football teams. The Department brought you up to be an individual, didn't they?"

"Yes," I admitted. I bit into the dumpling. It was soft and the pork filling was spicy.

"But you miss being we." Tears sprung to my eyes at the twins' empathy. Giang put her hand on my leg to comfort me. "We are glad you are here. At first, we missed having five and kept looking for the others. Then we learnt to be content with just two. But three is better. It's a time to be happy not sad."

Khanh took a swig of her champagne. In that moment I realised that the twins were as disconcerted as I was.

"Do you think… that we would murder too?"

"I don't think I would," I answered honestly. "But I do not think the animals are we."

"We are we," the twins chorused together, and we burst into bitter laughter.

"We're so glad we were fostered out of Việt Nam. Don't know how we would have stood being monitored all the time."

"It makes you more careful with what you say," I said. But the food is better, I thought.

I felt my cheeks go red with the champagne as we ate more pork dumplings. This was the joyful reunion I had been hoping for, which couldn't occur with Geraldine and Lien.

"I'm so happy to see you. I wish Lien and Geraldine could be here," I said.

Khanh and Giang looked at each other and then looked at me.

Giang cleared her throat.

"We know Geraldine is dying. We can feel her." She shuddered, and the twins held hands for comfort.

"It's not like that when you see her," I protested. "She's just sick, that's all."

"We dream that we are trapped in her body and are getting old and dying," Khanh explained. "It scares us. We dream about the other one too. She murdered someone. That's bad."

"Very bad," Giang said childishly. "Her nightmares are terrifying. We can't see them. We don't want to die or to kill anybody."

"You won't die if you see Geraldine. I didn't," I said.

"But you are…" Giang said.

"Alone," the two of them said together.

It was if a deep chasm had opened between us, a gulf of misunderstanding.

"You are not we," Khanh added.

Tears started to fill my eyes.

I am we… I began to say in my head but then stopped.

"Are the others we?" I asked indignantly.

Giang and Khanh looked at each other again.

"Once we were we. Then they separated us. When we are together, we feel like we again. We receive everything. You are upset by what we said. We are sorry.

"We are," they said again in unison and a shiver went down my spine. "If we are with Lien, we will become like her."

"I saw Lien and I'm nothing like her!" I retorted angrily.

"That's because you have been alone for so long. You are individuated. We are still we. We are not separate."

Then they nodded. Giang came over to me and hugged me. Then Khanh did the same, so we were linked in a group hug. I felt their apology and how sad they were that I was not we.

- *I am a little,* I thought at them and was startled to feel them react.

- Can you hear me?
- Yes.

Giang broke out into a smile.

- I can hear you but you are separate.

Happiness flooded me as we squeezed each other tighter.

- This is we.
- We are we.
- We are telepathic, I deduced.

Then we laughed again.

The twins had never been far apart in their lives. When they started primary school, well-meaning staff put them in separate classes. They stayed alone and silent in class then ran to each other's sides during recess and lunch breaks. When they were put together, they would contribute to their classes like ordinary kids. Khanh did most of the talking but Giang would provide the answers.

The twins did not want a relationship outside themselves. Their parents were a necessity for room and board, but left them alone when it became obvious, as they grew older, they were more independent of mind.

In high school one foolhardy boy asked Giang out. But Khanh was the one that showed up for the date. When he realised the switch, he was embarrassed and humiliated. No one from the school asked the twins for a date again.

The twins knew they were from a set of five.

Their parents told them the truth and said when they were twenty-five they would be told the identity of the other three. At first the twins were nonplussed. They had each other. What would they need the other three for?

But as they grew older, they became curious. If two was good, surely five would be better?

As they became technology-savvy they searched for the missing three. Their parents told them two were in Việt Nam and one was in Australia. The two in Việt Nam they soon found were untraceable from outside the country – the public records and information databases were patchy, ranging from classified secure to missing altogether. They were looking into enrolments at high schools in Sydney when they and their parents were hauled in for security reasons.

Their parents worked for CHESS and would lose their project funding if the girls contacted the other clones, and the girls would be taken away from their parents after voiding their worth as test participants. They had known better than to search the CHESS database itself, but they were not smart enough then, at age fifteen, to escape scrutiny.

Khanh and Giang understood. Their parents had told them they were special, being twins, and never hid from them that they were CHESS research subjects, with regular blood samples taken from them and the cognition tests they sat every so often.

Ma had five clones to run research on. They had tried to find her research but could not find anything at all, not even a sideways mention to indicate that something had been excised from the public record.

Khanh and Giang decided to play good so that they would be trusted.

As they neared twenty-five, they became excited yet scared. At twenty-four they were allowed e-mail contact with Geraldine. Geraldine was dying of cancer. This tempered their elation. They were told that Geraldine did not want video contact with them. She didn't want them to see her after chemotherapy had left her without hair.

It left them free to imagine what she looked like and what they feared. If they had the same genetic make-up, they had the potential for cancer too...

The twins became frightened. They asked for permission to see the other two before they all contracted a terminal illness.

To their relief and gratitude, the Department granted their request.

The twins thought they were the best out of all the clones, and to be polite tried to hide it from me. With their advanced telepathy, I could not argue with them.

After dumplings we decided to do a quick search on Khanh's computer. We clustered around the desktop, curious about the same things. Giang and Khanh had looked up Ma and her research. They told me Ma was dead, possibly having been executed by the Department.

- We don't know if there are other we.

They had scanned the net looking for other clone research, but all the official accounts still involved the cloning of animals, especially pets. There were too many debates about human cloning and the churches held sway in the Western countries.

Then we looked at research that involved identical twins and even triplets. No quadruplets or quintuplets, in respectable publications at least.

We remembered the blood tests every week and having what I now knew were psychological tests with structured play time and activities. Ma had been collecting our data for research. We wondered what for.

Most of the reported research was biomedical. Tests of vaccines and antibiotics.

No credible research involved psychic powers – those articles were left to be reported by the *Reader's Digest* and fake news outlets.

That closeness I felt with both Geraldine and Lien was psychic closeness. Geraldine and Lien were individuated as well, Khanh concluded.

- We will go to Việt Nam and visit Lien.

I raised my eyebrows. They did not mention Geraldine and I wondered at that. Were they so scared of dying?

- We don't want to feel her dying in our heads.
- We are not as strong as you.

For the first time I wondered whether the Department had inadvertently done the right thing in separating most of us.

Giang and Khanh looked at me in pity and I thought about a blank wall to hide behind. The downside to telepathy was rapidly becoming evident.

- We cannot see you behind your wall.

Khanh and Giang reached around and gave me a hug.

- We love you Vuong. Even though you need to hide from us behind a wall.

Sheepishly, I let the wall dissolve. I was scared, I admitted, as well as elated.

- Maybe the Department can tell us whether we will get cancer, Giang thought.
- Maybe. Evelyn might know. You realise they might want to monitor us all together, especially if they knew about tele…
- They don't know. It's our secret.

I was expecting to be gagged soon. The freedom they had was dizzying. It was all going well, too well. I put up the wall again and had another dumpling.

"Giang and Khanh are very close. Probably too close for my comfort. They were at pains to tell me that I was not we."

I let my discomfort show in front of Evelyn. According to my own thought experiments the telepathy disappeared when me and the twins were not in sight of each other. Despite my longing for we I was relieved.

I needed the privacy of my own mind.

"Are you disappointed?" Evelyn asked.

"I'm hurt, mostly," I lied. They had given me a present, a soft toy sheep. We all had soft toy collections, I realised, except Lien, who had nothing. I wondered how she would respond to telepathy, and suddenly I understood why the twins did not want to see Geraldine.

"What do you want to do when we are back?" Evelyn asked.

It was the first time a monitor had asked me what I wanted.

I seized the chance.

"I want to see all the medical and psychological records on the five of us and see the neurological and biological differences." We want to know if we will die of cancer, I thought.

"I may be able to access that now," Evelyn said.

"Have you been promoted?" My question came out unprompted.

"They may have cleared you to see the test results. These visits have gone very well. We may be able to get Geraldine and Lien a reunion."

I could not help the smile that came to my face. I was getting everything we wanted.

I could not wait to see Camille. She would be excited and appalled at the telepathy. I had pictures of Geraldine and the twins to show her. She would be glad that I was a reunited multiple.

I wondered whether I would still feel the same way about Camille now that I had felt the closeness of Giang and Khanh. Different, I told myself. The closeness was different even with empathy.

I had never been able to read Camille's mind.

Berlin – My

When I woke up my mother was in the kitchen making che dessert. My favourite.

"You have been sick," she said to me. "Freja and Truong brought you home."

My mother is a spy, I remembered. Then I remembered what Freja and Truong thought and the missing photo.

"I'm sorry, Ma," I said. I remembered what part I played in it too.

"You have nothing to be sorry for," she said, and a sense of wrongness came upon me. She was lying. I did not need empathy to read her, the words were strange enough. It was not like my mother to express such a sentiment.

"You just rest. We'll talk later," she told me.

She could not talk openly in our flat, I intuited. Maybe Truong could not talk with Freja present. My mind came up with plausible explanations. All were better than thinking I was going crazy.

And if I was, I would just not use empathy again. But the prospect of not feeling those experiences again made me bereft.

I closed my eyes and time seemed to shoot through me. I opened my eyes in the early morning and my mother was coming in from her shift.

I looked at her with new eyes. If she wasn't cleaning, what was she doing at CHESS every night?

She could be up to anything. I had never asked and never bothered to find out.

My mother came into my bedroom. Seeing I was awake, she sat on my bed and felt my forehead.

"You've been taking drugs with your friends," she said bluntly.

I nodded. There was no point denying it.

"What is it like? The empathy?" she asked.

"You feel love for everyone. And you feel other people's emotions." I saw an opportunity then. To influence her and the hui circle. "Like I felt how tired you are. But the come-down is huge. You feel empty of everything," I told her.

"Depressed?"

"Maybe," I hazarded a guess. I had never been depressed before. "Ma, are you ex-Stasi?"

"You've been affected by those drugs you take, My. You think this of everyone."

I looked at her knowingly. I hadn't told her what I had thought or said before about Truong being a drug supplier.

"After what you told me, you can trust me," I said. She looked at me strangely. "You can trust me. I know you are ex-Stasi."

"You've taken too many drugs. I don't know what to do about you."

She was close to tears. I felt her helplessness and desperation. And a steely resolve. But to do what?

"You don't have to do anything. I won't betray you. I won't go behind your back again. I promise."

"You need help," she said half to herself. She pulled herself together and the tears receded. "You need to see doctor," she told me briskly. "Wait for drugs to wear off."

"It's only empathy. It will wear off soon," I told her recklessly.

"Empathy. You don't know what it can do," she said and got her coat. "Come on," she said. When I was slow to move, she bundled me into my jacket. "You go see doctor with me. At private hospital. He is on shift."

"From your hui circle?"

"Yes, yes. From hui circle," she said impatiently as we walked briskly down the street. "Near Alexanderplatz."

Not the doctors at CHESS? My regular check-ups were with the doctors at CHESS.

My suspicions about what sort of hospital it was were confirmed when we stopped to turn into what looked like a mansion in grassy surrounds.

"Ma, I'm not crazy," I said as she rang the doorbell.

"You aren't crazy. Just drugged," she told me as the door opened.

"I'm here to visit Dr Mendes," she said to the Vietnamese receptionist who greeted us.

"He's on rounds. You are…"

"From his hui circle. Chi Nguyen."

"Okay. Take a seat. I'll page him."

We sat in the opulent waiting room, on plush blue couches. A television was playing silently in the background. It was showing a violent demonstration in Hamburg, neo-Nazis versus the police. Water cannons were firing into the crowd.

There had been an increase in these incidents, the tele-monitor scrolled.

A balding older Vietnamese man presented himself to us, neatly dressed in shirt and tie.

"Chi em." He greeted my mother with warmth, and I felt and saw the relief in her eyes.

"She is affected by empathy. She thinks I'm spying for the Vietnamese government and I'm ex-Stasi."

"Really?" Dr Mendes raised his eyebrows. They spoke in Vietnamese. "I can see how this would be a problem. Would you like her to stay here until she comes down?"

"Yes, please. I don't know what to do about her."

"She'll be safe here. Claire here can show her to a room while we have a chat."

"I'm staying here?" I felt numb.

"Just for one night," my mother said. "So you'll be sober from empathy. I can't look after you all day and I don't trust your friends to keep you clean…"

I picked up on her helplessness and hoped that she was doing the right thing. From Dr Mendes I only picked up concern.

I suddenly felt exhausted.

I went with the receptionist down a corridor to what looked like a hotel room. The room contained a clean single bed with white sheets, a cupboard and a bedside table. Brown curtains hid a window to the outside world.

"The doctor will see you shortly and your mother will say goodbye," the receptionist said. She gave me some brochures to look at as she closed the door.

It was better and worse than I thought. It was a facility for drugs and alcohol misuse. Not necessarily mad people, I thought.

My mother thought I was crazy. She had denied everything she had said to me before I caught up with Freja. It was true that what she had said had coincided with me coming down off empathy. But empathy fucked with your emotions, not your cognition, or so I thought. Ecstasy messed with both. It was possibly more complex even with the so-called higher-grade substances Truong was importing.

I had to get Truong alone, get the truth from him. I texted him where I was as my mother came by with Dr Mendes.

"A nurse will check your vitals and then you can sleep it off," Dr Mendes said. "The door isn't locked. You'll be checked upon hourly so you will be safe. There's a security camera on the corridor too. Breakfast at seven and you can check yourself out when you've come down. I will examine you again in the morning between eight and nine."

Dr Mendes let my mother give me a hug. I resisted her, even while flooded with her relief. Then she left and I sat down on the bed and the doctor sat down on a chair.

He asked me what time of day it was, and whether I could count backwards in threes from one hundred. Then he asked who had just left the room.

"My mother," I said, and I deliberately did not say anymore.

"Do you know why you are staying here?" he asked.

"My mother thinks I'm drug-affected by empathy."

"And have you taken any empathy in the last twelve hours?"

"Yes."

"Who is your supplier?"

"I'm not going to tell you that. He'll get in trouble," I said. Again I was speaking my thoughts aloud.

"What do you think of your mother?" he asked.

"I feel sorry for her."

"Have you done anything to upset her lately?"

I stared at him. Had my mother confided in this doctor what I did?

"She didn't know I took empathy until now."

He nodded, and I felt the sincerity of his concern, his bed-side manner.

"How are you feeling now?"

"Guilty," I said honestly. I had caused my mother all sorts of worry.

"Well, stay here until you come down. I'll review you in the morning."

He stood up and let himself out of the room.

I sat back on the bed, thinking hard. I did not confide in the doctor because I knew now it sounded crazy that my mother was ex-Stasi. Even Truong thought it was crazy. But he was a member of a hui circle that was part of a genuine conspiracy, or so I thought. I wanted proof from him, evidence that I wasn't losing my mind.

Saturation point was going to happen soon. And I needed to find out what that was. So I arranged to meet Truong at lunch, when the empathy should have cleared my system. I chose a café known for its coffee and croissants.

I went to sleep then and it was like blacking out. I opened my eyes and it was mid-morning.

Dr Mendes was as good as his word and let me sign myself out to leave. I texted my mother that I was out for lunch, and she texted back "Good." I figured she approved of Truong after he and Freja had taken me home. Not that it would have made any difference to me, Stasi or no Stasi.

When Truong arrived for coffee and met my eye I felt my attraction to him again. He was cute, I thought, even without empathy.

We sat at the small round café table with coffee, our legs touching.

"Are you okay?" he asked.

"Yes," I said. "I slept like the dead."

"Do you still think your mother is…"

"No," I lied. He could not handle the truth from me.

"I have a job for you," Truong said. "It's worth a lot of money and if you do it you won't need to work at the restaurant for a while."

"Is it legal?" I asked automatically. And was he for real this time?

"Technically it isn't illegal," he said. "I need a courier to take a sample of superior empathy to a hui circle contact in Hanoi. It will be in a generic tablet foil so it looks like aspirin, so you can just take it in your toiletries bag. The substance is not banned in Việt Nam so it's technically not illegal. If you're caught with it you won't get done for a prohibited substance."

"But in Germany…"

"It is. It's also patented by CHESS so it breaches intellectual property law to take it out of the laboratory. You're going to Hanoi in a week. I'll give you the contact's mobile and he'll tell you where to meet, probably in a tourist hotspot. I'll pay you half when you leave and half will be paid when you're in Việt Nam."

"And you trust me? Even after what I said about my mother?"

"I've dealt with paranoid people before. I know it's not you, it's the drug talking. You can try the drug I'm asking you to courier, I trust that you won't be stupid about it in Việt Nam. Your mother will be chaperoning you, I'll imagine, and I trust her to be a traditional mother in that sense. You're a nobody, no one would suspect you."

He was being so understanding I wanted to hit him out of frustration.

But with the money he was suggesting, I could treat myself and my mother like royalty in Việt Nam. I could help my mother – she always gave away more money than she could spare when she visited Việt Nam. All the relatives thought Việt Kiều were rich and she never disillusioned them with facts, she gave away lucky envelopes with chocolate and we stayed in good hotels in Hanoi. She dressed up too, in silk blouses and long trousers as a lady of leisure, while I just wore T-shirt and jeans, much to her despair.

But this time I could help. I would lie and say I had been saving up from the pay of the restaurant and my tips. I would also say I was meeting up with one of Truong's friends. Another lie.

And I would watch her every move. If she was ex-Stasi and a spy for the government, she would have to report to them somehow.

I would find out the truth.

I could not trust how she would react if I told her about the higher-grade empathy, spy or no spy.

"Do you trust your mother?"

Whether she was a spy or not, she was still my mother, I found myself thinking. I would protect her by not telling her about smuggling empathy. She did not need to know anymore.

"Yes, I trust her. As my mother."

I could not tell her about this or she would take me to the hospital again.

I couldn't take the risk.

As for this job, Truong had won me over with the money.

As he handed over a roll of euros it confirmed for me that this time it was for real.

Hanoi – Vuong

I got back to the apartment, carrying my travel bag, and opened the door.

When I saw Camille's silhouette my heart leapt. Then she looked at me and I knew something was wrong.

"Hello sweetheart. How are you?" I greeted her with a kiss.

"I'm all right. What was so classified that you couldn't tell me?"

Puzzled, I sat down next to her on the bed and told her about Geraldine, Giang and Khanh. As I spoke, I felt whatever it was that was bothering her growing. I hesitated and did not tell her about the telepathy I had experienced with the twins.

"And you're allowed to talk about them?" she asked me, holding my hand.

"No. But you are different. I trust you not to tell anyone else."

"You shouldn't," she said, cryptically, and the sense of something wrong, like a wrong note in music, struck me again.

"How have you been?" I asked.

"I'm fine," Camille said, uncomfortable.

"Are you okay with me being a multiple?" I was guessing now. Her discomfort was growing as we spoke.

"I'm fine with that. I just... can't be there for you the way that they can."

Plain, old-fashioned jealousy, I thought.

"I'd like you to meet them," I told her.

"I don't know if that will be allowed," she said.

"If they want all of us to co-operate with their research, they will need to let us do what we wish," I said more confidently than I felt.

Camille nodded. I felt the distance between us grow with each word I spoke. Something was definitely wrong.

"Camille, what's bothering you?"

Camille looked away.

"I work for the Department. I don't think you can rely on them to mean well." She seemed to come to some decision. Then she looked at me in the eye. "I report to them, Vuong," she said. "About you. You should not trust them."

"You report to them?" I was taken aback. "I thought you were an administrator..."

The bottom had fallen out of my world. More than meeting my multiples. Camille was my bedrock. No matter how weird the multiples were I could depend on Camille. At least I thought I could. But now…

"I do research too, Vuong. Since they are now disclosing everything to you I want to be open with you too. I do really love you, Vuong. I'm sick of being a spy for them. They told me you were a multiple just after I met you. I was broke and I wasn't earning much as a research assistant in the Department."

Words came tumbling out of her mouth like river stones.

She was desperate, I perceived.

"Why are you telling me this? Why now?" I demanded.

"You deserve the truth, Vuong. I'm sorry. I truly am."

"I can't talk to you," I muttered. That was why she had accepted me being a multiple so easily. She already knew. She had known all along.

"I'm sorry. I really am sorry." Tears were welling in her eyes.

A sense of disbelief cascaded over me along with a terrible acceptance of the truth.

"Can't talk now!" I yelled and ran from our apartment.

I found myself on the train to the Department.

I wanted to confront Evelyn. Confirm Camille's deception. Then maybe I would know what to do with her.

What I would do with me.

I felt dirty and sickened. The Department had manipulated me all my life. Nothing was untouched by it.

I held on to the telepathy with Giang and Khanh. It was the only secret we had left.

We are still we, I thought to myself in a tiny voice.

Camille's confession made me run over everything she had said to me in a new light. Her easy acceptance of me being a multiple – too easy. She had always known. Known me better than I knew myself.

When I got off the train Evelyn was waiting for me at the platform. Confirming Camille's co-operation with them. She must have informed them of my leaving. Or they have a tracker in my phone. What was more likely, I did not know anymore.

"Vuong," Evelyn began.

"Evelyn…" I didn't need her fake sympathy.

"We need to take this inside," Evelyn said and gripped my arm with pincer-tight fingers. I let myself be dragged along into the grey building, past the security guards.

"I want Camille removed," I said in the lift. The display flicked up to Level 5.

"You can request that," Evelyn said neutrally. "But is it really what you want? You wanted to see the records on you five. I'm about to take you to the archive so you can view whatever you want."

"Why now?" I asked. Good things never happened without a reason. They were trying to distract me.

"Your self-reports are what are useful to the Department. We need to know what your maturation has been like. From the inside. We need to know if you… are well balanced and functioning as well as you could be."

"Why? Are you making more of us?"

"We haven't yet assessed all the risks. There have been other illegal multiples but none as well researched as you five. We have the cleanest data set on multiples in the world."

She stepped out of the lift and I followed her. We entered a data room and I sat down in a black chair, folding my arms in front of the projection monitors.

Evelyn drew up a link list of data titled "Multiple" and I scanned it quickly.

The table was dry, listing names of neurological functions and dates of video archive files. It became more interesting near the end, comparisons of our five brain functionings and reports from psychologists, psychiatrists and neuroscientists.

Hesitantly, I wondered about whether the original was marked in the data.

I flicked up a series of scans at random. They were numbered one through five. Evelyn had been as good as her word. I had the data but none of the conclusions that accompanied it.

"Where are the self-reports?" I asked.

"It's not in your interest to see those. The others need to consent for you to see them."

I stilled my initial angry response. I needed Evelyn's co-operation.

"Is there a summary report of everything that is here?"

Evelyn highlighted a link and pulled it up for me. I wanted to know if they knew about our telepathy.

I skipped to the end of the summary.

With morbid curiosity I read about myself. I was social, engaging and had normal affect. Perhaps an oversensitivity to others, which may have been due to the use of empathy.

They had concluded that staged re-introduction could work now that we were all old enough. There were volumes on Khanh and Giang and comparisons between them, Lien, myself and Geraldine.

I read the observations of me. I realised that the point of view was Camille's and I felt sick in the stomach. I felt vulnerable and transparent like glass.

We had been exploited.

I read and read. Buried among measurements of serotonin and dopamine were readings about neurochemical similarities between the five of us. Khanh and Giang were almost identical. But compared to a random population distribution, all five of us had profiles that were as good as identical. They were particularly high in the areas related to empathy.

Then to my surprise the report ended with a "commercial in confidence" code.

"What is this?" I asked.

"The patent has been approved so it's commercial in confidence," Evelyn said uncomfortably. "My clearance doesn't go that high."

I thought about what to say next without mentioning the word telepathy.

"Patent for what?" Evelyn was silent. "Come on! Have you been using us as lab rats even though we weren't old enough to give informed consent?" I shouted.

"Ssssh!" Evelyn came to sit next to me.

"Empathy," she whispered in my ear.

"*What?*"

"Empathy. They developed it from your chemistry profiles. Then patented it. I don't know what's in it. Other labs have tried to make similar drugs. But they don't have our data."

I stared at her. I wanted to hit her. All those tests. The Department would make billions from the patent of empathy.

"That's why you've kept multiples secret! In case another country develops empathy!"

"It's not the only thing. Your identical genetic codes mean we've been able to isolate many variables in neurochemistry. Better psychotherapeutic drugs that have helped millions…"

"What about us? How about helping us? Lien is a nutcase and if we had been with her she may not have killed her foster father…"

"We are helping her. With empathy and other drugs. She will be rehabilitated."

"It's a bit late for her father! And now we are mature you can let us go," I added.

"Neuroplasticity means we are interested in monitoring you until death – but full consent is required. You are all old enough now. You are no longer wards of the Department. We also need you to co-operate to produce the more meaningful results with the psychological tests we use."

"So you need us all now. That's why you let us be we. You need us to be grateful test subjects."

"Participants, Vuong. There are some neurochemical reactions we can't observe with unknowing people. We need to know what happens when you think and react in certain ways to given stimuli. We've gone as far as we can go observing passively. You will be paid more than enough to live on. All five of you. You can live together. Even with Camille, if you want to."

"I don't want…" I stopped myself in time.

"You now have access to sensitive information. Even before our international partners protocol has been established. The West is precious about intellectual property and patents. They do not believe in the common good. It makes collaboration difficult when they do not want to share what little they have. To save face the Department won't share either, so no one wins. International collaboration is more about politics than science." Evelyn sighed. "I can give you some time to think about it, Vuong. And you can talk to some people that may help you."

The entrance of the data room opened. Khanh and Giang were escorted in by security.

"Giang and Khanh are in particular very special to the empathy project. Their data set forms the basis of our neurochemical understanding of empathy."

It made sense. It all made sense.

"I'll leave you three to catch up," Evelyn walked out with security, leaving us alone.

"They greeted us at the airport," Khanh explained.

- *Are you okay?* Giang asked.

Khanh and Giang embraced me, heedless of the security camera in the room.

- *Talk aloud. So they don't suspect...*

"What happened? What's this?" Giang glanced over the summary report.

"It's about us..." Khanh was riveted by the sentences of the discussion.

- *They created empathy by studying we.*
- *What?*
- *They created empathy by studying our neurochemistry.*

"Why have they done this?" asked Khanh aloud.

"Because they could. They had the power and resources to test empathy with us." I had slipped up. It was too hard separating thoughts from verbal words.

The sliding door to the data room opened and Evelyn came back in.

"You multiples are astute and smart women. That's why we need you on-side. To fully research empathy on willing participants. Empathy is more than an aphrodisiac. It makes people feel how other people feel. It negates aggression and promotes understanding. We can use it to make peace. As we briefed Khanh and Giang here."

An inkling of what she was talking about dawned on me then. The effects of Khanh and Giang on me. From individual to large-scale. And I was horrified.

"Chemical warfare," Khanh said.

"No. The opposite of warfare. We have seeded water supplies with empathy. And thousands of people take empathy regularly of their own free will."

"But it's only been around for five years…" I said.

"Only commercially available for five years. We've had ample time to test it in Việt Nam and do what needs to be done."

"You're pacifying whole populations with empathy!" I exclaimed. My anger had found a target. I had been manipulated and used for the last time.

"Not pacifying. We are accelerating altruism and empathy for others. The human race has not outgrown its aggressive capacity in time to preserve lives."

"So what do you need us for now?" I asked. "More tests?"

"We need you for observation and for you to design and run different tests to better develop empathy and other medications. You five are very special. We can set you up in a large house with four bedrooms overlooking the lake. You will be reporting in every so often but you will not be monitored."

"You would set Lien free?"

"Yes. She is best rehabilitated with you others. She will have a monitoring bracelet but that is all. You will receive a salary. You can tell other people that you are sisters and cousins."

It was everything I wanted. But Camille...

My mind shied away from thinking about Camille. Instead, I thought about the Department. I did not want to be a lab rat for the rest of my life.

- Shush now. We are citizens of Aotearoa. Just go along with them for now.

I glanced at Khanh, who was the more insightful and dominant of the two. I knew that even without reading the report on the twins.

"You may want to talk it over with Camille," Evelyn said.

I stared into space, clenching my jaw till my teeth hurt. Giang put her arm around me and I felt the comfort of we.

'We will come with you if you like," Khanh said, reading my mind.

I flinched.

- We are we, Giang and Khanh thought together contentedly.

Isn't this what I wanted? I thought. The reality was very different to my wishes and dreams. Childishly, I hid behind my wall as Evelyn escorted the three of us out of the data room and from the building.

HANOI – MY

I spent the next few days away from the club scene, drying out from empathy. The effects seemed to drain the world of bright colours, but I found my muted senses relaxing and comforting rather than boring after the amplification I had experienced on empathy. I rested up. It was my second visit to Việt Nam, and I prepared myself for sensory overload.

My mother seemed to be normal, going about her shifts and saying and doing nothing that alluded to espionage or empathy. She appeared to have forgiven me and did not mention my breaking her trust at all. It made me feel all the more guilty, and the thought that I was smuggling empathy to Việt Nam made me feel worse.

But the money enticed me and she would benefit, I told myself.

Our flight was delayed by a couple of hours. Rumour had it that someone had not appeared for boarding, so they had to remove her luggage from the plane to make sure it wasn't a bomb. They were being extra-careful.

"Damned terrorists," my mother said. "It's the Africans and the Afghans," she continued, conflating all the so-called terrorist groups she knew.

I looked around, embarrassed, but no one seemed to notice. For a moment I doubted that my mother could be sophisticated enough to be Stasi. Then I remembered how even among my own friends there was intolerance and ignorance of refugee groups.

Our luggage was packed to the limits. The extra aspirin pack was in my bath bag in my hand luggage. I was not tempted to try one yet. Dealing with immigration, German and Vietnamese, made me nervous enough.

"I wouldn't have thought Việt Nam would have its own home-grown terrorists," my mother continued as we boarded our flight. "They aren't a target for Arabs. And there's no Muslims in Việt Nam."

I didn't contradict her, I just let her rattle on. She was anxious and she talked to distract herself. But I suddenly paid attention when she mentioned CHESS.

"I got a long-service award from CHESS. A certificate and a bonus. We both have money to spend in Việt Nam. We can try all the European fusion places. Take our family to the five-star restaurants."

I was caught up in her enthusiasm. She was as privileged as a queen in Việt Nam.

Suddenly I wondered. Did my mother ever want to come back and live in Việt Nam?

She hesitated, and I realised I had yet again spoken thoughts aloud. These slippages were embarrassing.

"I would like to, one day. But what about you?" she asked.

"I don't want to live in Việt Nam," I replied too quickly. I took a breath. "But I'm twenty-five now. I can move out and you can live in Hanoi if you want to."

Inside I felt something inside me give way. I wanted my mother to be happy. Even if it meant she wasn't living with me or in the same country.

She smiled, tears in her eyes, and I hugged her. The closeness I felt then was the most I had ever felt to my mother, and all without empathy.

We caught an airport hotel shuttle and I saw my mother draw herself up as she directed the driver to take our bags. She was taller and the driver deferred to her authority. I just followed her lead and let her do all the talking.

We were in one of the five-star hotels, which we would never have been able to afford in Berlin. To my delight, it had a pool and both Vietnamese and Western breakfasts.

I sprawled out in the blessed air-conditioning, the tropical air making me relax and sweat at the same time.

"We go out see cousins," my mother said after a shower. We shared a twin room with two queen-size beds. She saw no need for privacy, so neither did I.

We jumped on the backs of two xe ôms and I gloried in the reckless moped traffic that was the norm in the crowded streets of Hanoi. Thirty kilometres an hour without a helmet on a xe ôm packed with people or luggage like chickens or a fridge. Everything to marvel at through the Western eye.

We went further out of the central district to my cousins' house. It was a narrow four-storey dwelling. Properties were taxed by width so people built up instead of across.

My closest cousins were the children of my mother's cousins. My mother had lost most of her direct relatives in the American War and treasured the ones that were left. On the last visit I had felt little affinity with my cousins. They were younger than me by three years, but at least now we might have music in common. And they were old enough to drink, I speculated as we were greeted at the door. Maybe we could hang out together...

Dai greeted me in slender-leg jeans and tight T-shirt. She looked much the same as when I saw her last.

"Hello, German," she said, and gave me a hug.

"Hi. How's things?"

"Hot. Even for me."

She led the way into the house while my mother was accosted with much oohing and ahhing by two older aunts.

"You so skinny. You never get a man with chopstick legs," my aunt pinched my wrist. "You on a diet? Share it with Dai. She eats too much food."

Dai propped up a smile and I felt her shame as if it were my own.

The empathy was still leaving an emotional residue, I detected. That, or I had grown to like my cousin who I hadn't seen for two years real quick. The side effects came at random times. Maybe it took time for the empathy to completely clear your system.

"We go play," she told the aunts and took my wrist, dragging me outside.

She straddled a pink moped and motioned for me to hop on.

I did so obediently, telling myself I could spy on my mother later.

We went back into the tourist district and parked by Hoan Kiem Lake. She took me to have ice cream and then for dinner. At first I went along with it – I genuinely was curious as to how she was. But it became evident she wasn't going to go home, and she viewed my time and presence as hers alone.

"You're so lucky in Berlin," she said. "Western countries are so free. You can do whatever you like. You can have sex whenever you like. Don't you?"

Even though it was true, I was still taken aback by her bluntness.

"I can," I said.

"It's hard to get condoms and the pill. It's embarrassing. Would you be able to get some for me? You're Việt Kiều, they would expect you to want some…"

"Do you have a boyfriend?" I asked.

She blushed.

"Sort of," she admitted. He was a university student, twenty years old. Her parents didn't know. We would be meeting him in half an hour.

Suddenly I knew why she was monopolising my time. I was a cover for her to spend time with her boyfriend.

Feeling used, I told her I was tired and wanted to go back to the hotel.

"I'll catch a xe ôm," I said. When I hugged her, I felt shame and relief.

I checked my rising frustration at my unpredictable feelings. The empathy was manipulating me this way. I could not stay mad at people.

The xe ôm driver was simply happy he had snagged a fare.

A couple of Vietnamese tourists were sitting in the foyer reading the newspaper as I entered the hotel.

When I got back to our room, I took out the tablet foil of empathy and stared at it for a moment. This was higher-grade, quality stuff.

More pacifying? Would I wish this on anyone?

I remembered the good sex I'd had. Which hadn't been for a few days.

I looked at the perforated foil packaging. I tore one of the tabs off and put the single sample back in my bath bag. I would keep this for myself as proof, I thought. I wasn't sure what for, but I needed confirmation of reality.

I pulled up the contact's number on my phone and texted him the message Truong had asked me to say.

Hi. I'm here. Let's meet up sooner rather than later.

The reply was immediate.

About time. By the one-pillar pagoda next to the tiger.

Truong had arranged a drop-off spot only three blocks away from our hotel.

The couple of tourists were still reading the paper as I walked out of the hotel foyer. I concentrated on the busy streets, avoiding the constant moped traffic with the incessant honking. So I did not realise I was being followed until two blocks had gone by.

I felt a prickle down my skin. I looked over my shoulder at a man in a short-sleeved shirt and trousers walking deliberately through the traffic towards me.

I kept walking. The one-pillar pagoda was up ahead, with the tiger on its façade. People milled around the entrance. I could not tell who was waiting for whom in the crowd.

My phone buzzed.

Walk around the lake.

I obeyed. The man behind me was not subtle. As I went along the path, he followed.

My skin crawled. Then I saw another man in the crowd of people following the man who was tailing me. We went a handful of steps together and then my pursuer detoured and walked away from me. He was followed by the second man into the traffic.

From sheer inertia I kept walking and told myself not to burst into a run.

I wanted to go back to the hotel, but someone could follow me back.

A text message chimed for me.

Trust me on the moped.

As if reading my mind, a xe om pulled up beside me. It was the second man.

"I lost the security agent. They hate being followed," my contact said grinning. "Come. We'll go somewhere less conspicuous."

His bravado reminded me of Truong, and he wasn't bad-looking either.

He motioned for me to sit behind him on the moped.

We went into the side streets and pulled into what looked like a shed where they were serving pho. Catering for the locals, it was 12,000 dong for a large bowl, and we perched on baby plastic chairs on the pavement.

"Have you got what we came for?"

I produced the box from my bag and gave it to him.

A sense of relief hit me then as he put the box away in his shirt pocket.

"How long are you here for?" he asked.

"A week," I told him.

"Plans?"

"Seeing my relatives. Nothing much. I've done most of the tourist stuff."

"I can take you clubbing. The empathy here is expensive for Vietnamese but nothing to foreigners."

I perked up at the thought of clubbing.

After pho we went to a busy street front where rows of mopeds were parked.

An entrance cut out of an aluminium roller door opened out to the street and two bouncers stood by casually as we went in. The inside was a mise en scène of dim multi-coloured lights. The bass rhythm thumped my ear drums as we paid at the door. It was marginally cooler inside the club and I headed straight for the bar. Huu came with me and ordered beers.

Then he produced two diamond-shaped pills.

I palmed one and swallowed it with my beer.

The taste of the tablet was familiar, reassuringly so. I waited for the effects as we headed for the dance floor. I reminded myself that I wasn't going to have sex with anyone in Việt Nam. I hadn't prepared for it with contraception or condoms for myself.

Just surf the feelings, I told myself as we danced.

I became aware that Huu was a good dancer. He moved his body in time to the music. He was lithe and intense, his body close to mine.

I found myself kissing him and a surge of desire overcame me, his desire all at once. Inside my head my reluctance was drowned by a desperate urge to fuck.

He grabbed my hand and took me off the dance floor. We went into the back where there were a series of cloak rooms. A hostess approached us and Huu gave her some money. We took a room and my mouth melted with his touch.

We fucked and I orgasmed as well as I had with Truong. Truong was who I thought of as we made love, the only comparison I could make.

Only when we were sated did I realise I had had unprotected sex.

But I was so blissed-out it didn't seem to matter.

"I'll escort you back to your hotel," he said.

I let him, my natural caution shot to hell.

I quietly let myself into my hotel room and had a shower. When I touched my skin, I had a pleasurable echo. I fell into a trance-like sleep.

I woke up and I was in Truong's arms, sated with after-sex sleep. The smell of his sweat was reassuringly familiar, as was his stirring against me as he opened his eyes. Then I closed my eyes again.

But when I woke up in the morning I was in Hanoi, on my own in my hotel bed, desolate. Half of my payment for being a mule was stuffed in American dollars in my jeans.

I had not done what I had set out to do. I felt used. It was not my desire that had driven my actions last night.

I had had unprotected sex with someone I could not trust.

What was wrong with me?

I had not stayed faithful to Truong. Not that we had talked about it. We didn't even have an understanding as such. I didn't even know how I would feel if he slept with some-one else. We were casual about our sex, enhanced as it was with empathy.

Bloody empathy, I thought as I got dressed.

I felt bad about the night before. It seemed like a dream now. This was a side of empathy I had not anticipated. I felt a sudden responsibility, being the courier of that high-quality sample. What would a higher grade of empathy do?

A mass orgy? Make women more compliant?

Illicit drugs were never about ethics, I knew that. But if my mother was involved in this surely she thought she was doing something good – or did she?

Was I?

I had not wanted to think too much about it before. But after last night I veered away from thinking about the possible consequences of my actions.

I knew if I had not couriered the drug someone else would have, or so I told myself.

Maybe I could influence my mother and Truong and find out more about what they were planning. Find out about saturation point.

Coming to this conclusion let me relax a little.

I went downstairs for breakfast, where mother was already sitting reading a newspaper.

"You played late with friend," was all she said to me in greeting.

Then I accompanied her on her round of visits to our relatives.

I waited all day to see if my contact would try to reach me again.

He didn't, confirming the casual nature of our encounter to him.

I watched my mother for any unusual contacts. One of my great aunts was a money lender but she was upfront about it, even asking my mother if she wanted a share in an international hui circle.

It was in the late afternoon around cups of tea that one of my aunts started talking politics. We had already been there for an hour and I had already tuned out after seemingly inexhaustible gossip about all my extended family.

She made mention of the premier wanting to pacify the Chinese over the South Sea. My mother commented that the situation was difficult, and I suddenly paid attention. She never talked about Vietnamese politics to me. Maybe now she was sharing with me because I was growing up.

"China is difficult to infiltrate," my mother said. "We can access them through their students overseas and their artists in Berlin."

Suddenly the whole day was made worthwhile. She had confirmed my suspicions.

"We are making inroads and the drug is popular. The street quality is improving too. The CHESS leak worked. We've almost reached saturation point."

I gulped. Was I part of a larger sting operation? I suddenly felt naive and out of my depth. How much did my mother know?

Saturation point referred to the penetration of empathy in the drug market, then.

I looked at her then and my mother glanced at me knowingly, I thought.

Suddenly I wanted to confess all. Make it up to her. I had betrayed her trust. But I couldn't here. Not in front of these women. I didn't know who they were.

Then I pulled myself up as she poured more tea.

Was I being paranoid?

I blinked.

"Young Dzung has been promoted to assistant secretary in the UN Vietnamese office," another woman said proudly, and was congratulated all round. "He'll be in Berlin for the UN Security Council meeting next week."

"My has finished her degree with honours," my mother said, and again the congratulations to her and me.

I smiled uncomfortably.

No one seemed to have noticed the sudden change in topic. Were they performing for eavesdroppers or spies?

If so, they were doing a superb job of gossiping boring minutiae.

They mentioned the Security Council meeting in Berlin. It coincided with Drei, the three-day dance party and the socialist street protests.

Was penetrating that scene with empathy their way of ensuring peace?

I blinked and my mother was rising, thanking auntie for the tea. She gave her a lucky money packet and received an effusive hug goodbye.

I was tired and wanted to be back in the hotel room.

I blinked and was back in my hotel bed.

Hanoi – Vuong

On the train back to my apartment the twins were fascinated by the green rice paddy fields and the rural life down below the tracks. They let me sit alone as I stewed over what I had been told. Potentially empathy could make the whole human race feel for each other, whether they liked it or not. There was something wrong with that, I thought. I worried about Lien. She was a prisoner of the Department. They could do anything to her.

- *We will tell the whole story of us multiples*, Giang said. *Both me and Khanh will go to the media. Then they will have to stop what they are doing with the water.*
- *We can produce the reports on us*, Khanh said. *We just need a computer.*

I raised my eyebrows at we. The twins were not just secretaries, I was beginning to realise. They were too smart for administration.

We got off at our platform and my stomach began to ache from the tension. I felt a moment of freedom being out of the Department which was replaced by resentment and frustration at Camille.

What was I going to say to her?

I barely noticed that Khanh and Giang were walking behind me, leaving me to my own thoughts. We reached the building and ascended in the lift to our floor.

Giang and Khanh flanked me and gave me a hug. Their kindness brought tears to my eyes.

– *We are we,* the twins thought together and I managed a smile.

I swiped my keycard on the lock and walked into our studio. Camille was sitting there hunched over, and I saw that she had been crying.

Something melted inside of me and I went over to her, sitting beside her.

Giang and Khanh stood by the door like sentinels. They were giving me space again, I realised.

"Thank you for telling me the truth," I said to her gently. Somehow being around Giang and Khanh made my anger dissipate. Their care and kindness made my resentment dissolve.

"I'm so sorry," Camille said. She wiped her eyes and glanced at Giang and Khanh. Then she did a double take and looked at them again.

"They look like you," she said inadequately.

"We are we," Giang told her. "Nice to meet you."

"I'll make some tea," Camille offered and the twins smiled at her. I was buoyed by their acceptance, as gentle as empathy.

"With what you know you could bring down the Department," Camille suggested as we drank tea and ate biscuits.

"The government would find other ways to carry on. Just not covertly like they have been," Khanh said.

- I won't tell her about our telepathy. It should just be for we.

I didn't know if I could trust her again.

- We agree, the twins said.

We are we. Even Camille's presence did not totally wreck my mood. I still was reserved with her – I could not go back to the trust I had in her previously. But my anger was gone, courtesy of we. It made me realise how potent empathy could be in changing mood and aggression. I felt soft, easily manipulated by the Department through Camille. But somehow Giang and Khanh's acceptance and presence made me feel a sense of wellbeing regardless.

It made me uneasy that my moods were that pliable to the twins. Something somewhere in our shared neurochemistry was the active compound for empathy. I was experiencing it firsthand without any synthetics. The effects did not seem to wear off, unlike the tablet form.

- We see Lien tomorrow. Do you want to come with us to our hotel?
- Yes.

"I'm going to stay with Giang and Khanh tonight. We're seeing Lien tomorrow."

"When will I see you again?" Camille was trying not to beg. "I need to warn you, Lien has gotten worse…"

"How do you know…" The full implications of her being an agent for the Department hit me then, opening like a terrible flower. Anger at her sprung out from me. I wanted to strangle her pretty little neck for betraying we. She would have told them everything, my reactions, my thoughts.

I hissed and Khanh caught my hands.

"Vuong! We're going now!"

I was propelled out the door. Giang fetched my unopened overnight bag.

I did not trust myself to speak, my rage had surprised me as well. It was as strong as Lien's. I could murder, I thought, and I felt the twins recoiling from the thought.

- We all could murder given the right triggers, Giang thought as we went to catch a taxi to the tourist district.
- And we all could have developed cancer, Khanh added. *And be telepathic to each other.*

I breathed deeply, hands shaking. I let Khanh and Giang hold me by the arms. They soothed me, calming me down by hugging me. I bathed in their peace.

When we reached the hotel, I was my normal reticent self again. But I was no longer alone.

I wasn't surprised to learn that they had never had intimate relationships with anyone else. They only had an intellectual inkling about Camille and me – it was inconceivable to them to be so close to someone and still betray them.

- *Camille is not in your head,* Giang said bluntly, heedless of my feelings.

Fearing what could happen with Lien, I taught Giang and Khanh how to imagine a wall around each other and be separate from me and one another. If I could fly into a psychotic rage without being near Lien, so could they.

They found it hardest to be separate from each other and did not like it.

"We are we," Khanh said, putting up a wall that hid her and Giang from me.

"We have always been together," Giang said.

I took a separate hotel room, and when I was alone was able to cry. Not only for Camille and me, but for Lien and Geraldine. The whole sorry mess.

The enormity of what we were and what the Department had made from us and about us was still dawning on me. They would never let us go and be normal – or what passed for normal. I wanted normal things, a girlfriend, a good job.

Who would want to go out with a fucking clone?

Away from the comfort of Giang and Khanh I had nothing. But even just thinking about them made me feel at peace.

I still had we. And if we could calm my rage at Camille what could Giang and Khanh do for Lien?

I pushed aside the larger question about the effect of empathy on a large population. It was too big to think about. They had been doing it for years and Việt Nam seemed much the same – maybe more capitalist, which was scarcely an empathy-driven direction.

My mind went over my relationship with Camille, all our interactions and conversations about the Department. She would have reported it all, my hostility, my reactions to Lien. I felt dirty and used. Nothing was sacred except for Giang and Khanh. Was Camille's affection a lie too?

She said she was approached after we started going out. I didn't want to trust her or care for her anymore. Instead, I concentrated on we.

When I finally drifted off to sleep, I was wrapped in the embrace of we, imagining us as we had been when we were four years old, crowded into a double bed, nice and warm.

Giang, Khanh, Geraldine, Lien and me. There were only the five of us and Ma. We didn't need anyone else and we were content and happy.

Berlin – My

When I woke up I was back in the coolness of the hospital bed in Berlin.

I was not in Hanoi.

The room was empty except for me and my small overnight bag.

I blinked and I was awake in the air-conditioned room in Hanoi, sweaty and uncomfortable. I stirred and moved.

I blinked again and I was back in the clinic in Berlin. I was groggy and sedated. It must have been something in the water – I didn't remember taking any drugs, legal or illegal.

Was I here or there?

My Hanoi memories were recent, like episodes of Netflix or TV. I closed my eyes and was back in hot, sweaty Hanoi again.

My mother took me and our relatives to the best restaurants in Hanoi, which catered for wealthy locals as well as overseas visitors. We even had turtle at a five-star restaurant with local seafood, which I paid for over my mother's insistence that she pay for everything.

I enjoyed the food even though my senses were dull coming off empathy. I rode on my mother's excitement of being in Hanoi – she was alive in a way that she was not in Berlin. She did not seem to be engaged in any further espionage-like activities as far as I could make out. Without this further confirmation of my suspicions my desire to tell her what I had done began to fade.

She could have done her business when I was out with my cousin. I could not know for sure.

The package was out of my hands now. There was nothing more I could do, I told myself as I prepared to go to sleep after a late-night supper with my mother and more relatives.

I fell asleep and woke up in Berlin. This time my head was clear, and I was certain. My mother was ex-Stasi. I had nothing to go on but my intuition. I had to tell Truong. The three-day dance festival was coming up, Drei, and the empathy infiltration would be at saturation point. Drei was at the same time as the UN Security Council meeting. The empathy would influence the decisions made there.

I had to tell Truong he was being used. He had to believe me this time.

Energised, I got dressed and went to breakfast. After a cold ham-and-cheese roll, I packed my overnight bag and signed myself out. No one tried to stop me, much to my surprise. I was truly a voluntary admission.

There was a chill in the air. I felt it on my cheeks, a contrast to my recollections of Hanoi. The colours were muted too. Winter in Berlin was dreary without empathy.

I headed towards Truong's flat. I wondered what I would do if I found him with another woman.

I banged on his door. He didn't come immediately, and I wondered whether I would have to hunt him down when he opened the door.

He was alone, I intuited to my relief, and his smile made it all worthwhile.

"Where have you been? Your mother wouldn't tell me where you were... I knew you were back from Hanoi..."

"Clinic," I said and recalled that I didn't actually know for how long. Not more than a few days, I thought, but...

"They wouldn't let me see you," he explained.

"They didn't tell me you stopped by," I said. Or they did and I hadn't remembered.

"That doesn't matter. You're here. Come in. How are you?"

I edged into his flat and sat on a clear spot on the couch.

"Good. I think. I've lost a couple of days and I think it's the empathy I took over there..."

"A couple of days? They use a purer product in Việt Nam, it's cheaper there. How did your mum cope with it?"

"She didn't know... I don't think..." The more I looked back on it, the more unlikely it was that she did not know I was drug-affected. Who admitted me to the clinic? Had it been me? "Empathy is a scary drug, Truong. Even though it's fucked with my mind I still want more of it. And in Việt Nam they are using it to pacify the population. They are going to pacify Berlin at Drei at the same time as the UN Security Council meeting."

Truong's eyes widened in concern, I thought, at what I was saying.

"You think that empathy is being used as a drug to pacify Berliners."

"And the UN staff and ambassadors and diplomats." I could see the audaciousness of it all and how wide the influence of the drug could spread from some partygoing UN staffers and their children.

"My, I'm worried about you. The empathy you took has really messed with your mind big time."

"Yes, I know. I'm not crazy though – it's true! My mother was discussing saturation points in regard to different populations! Their biggest challenge is influencing China! The Western countries are easy!"

As I said it, it made more and more sense. But I could tell from the look in his eyes that I had lost Truong.

I could tell the media…

In the meantime, I gave Truong a kiss. We made love then and it was ordinary. I deliberately flashed back to when we were on empathy and I got an echo of what it was like before, but only a small effect. From Truong's rueful smile I imagined he was doing the same thing.

"I still love you," he murmured, and I did a double take. His eyes were closed and a small snore escaped his lips.

"Me too," I whispered back from the crook of his shoulder, not knowing what I meant. Something had to remain a mystery.

I went home then. My mother greeted me with joy and relief and made me congee to eat, which she only did when I was sick. Which I had been, in a way.

I did not tell her I was missing recollections of us returning home from Hanoi – I didn't want to scare her. She just seemed to be my mother, readying herself for another cleaning shift at CHESS.

After our hotel room in Hanoi, our apartment seemed large with its kitchen and lounge room. Mother had never aspired for anything more as far as I knew.

I decided to post the truth on social media. I wrote a short blog piece on how empathy was pacifying the population and in particular how the dance party Drei coincided with the UN Security Council meeting in Berlin.

"Read like this, it sounds a bit farfetched," Truong told me.

"That's how come the conspiracy is so effective," I explained to him.

I hadn't told Freja in advance – she would just say I was hallucinating again.

Truong said nothing further, he just watched as I posted the link on Facebook and Twitter.

Within half an hour I had gotten comments.

From people who wanted to know where they could get good empathy at Drei.

No one picked up on the social engineering aspect of my piece. It was ignored.

Disappointed and frustrated, I wondered what I could do next. If anything.

I sent the article to all the media outlets and only a left-leaning radical site that published anti-vaccination articles and conspiracy theories bothered to e-mail me back. It published the article but with a disclaimer saying it did not reflect the site's views.

I did not know whether I had done myself a disservice or not, publishing with them. No one was prepared to draw the same conclusions or believe me.

It only registered attention as fake news.

On the first day of the UN Security Council meeting, I could not stay away from the protest lines outside the cordon at Potsdamer Platz. The usual suspects were there, left-leaning socialists and Marxists, with the occasional Anarchist, some in black-cloaked masked costumes like those in *V for Vendetta*. Standing in line two or three deep facing the cordon of still policemen and security barricades, they were holding up signs but were not chanting. In fact, they were swaying and singing softly instead.

It was a benign protest, far from the immigration protest's atmosphere at Alexanderplatz.

It was like being at a festival rather than a demonstration. There was none of the anger and protest I was used to feeling at rallies. Even the visible police presence seemed tokenistic, observing rather than intimidating. The police leant on their riot shields rather than having them battle-ready. They were chatting among themselves.

We signed a petition and walked away unharassed by either side.

Maybe the saturation point wasn't such a bad thing, I thought to myself. If it engendered peace...

There were no arrests made or reports of violence around the protests at the UN summit.

Motions were passed that experts predicted would be deadlocked. Member states that were locked in position had moved towards more peaceful outcomes. Germany in particular had moved, and so had China, along with its allies. Việt Nam too.

China had backed off its claims to the South Sea, seceding to Việt Nam to everyone's surprise.

"Empathy?" I asked Truong as I scrolled down the newspaper feed from the UN.

"Does it matter what caused it?" Truong commented back. "Peace and good will to all men."

"And women," I added.

I was resigned to being disbelieved now. At least Truong did not think I needed to be locked up and I wasn't going to disturb my mother anymore. She had worried enough about me. It would benefit no one if I outed her as being a spy.

I returned home to have dinner with her before her night shift at CHESS.

"How is work?"

"It is work, it is money," she said.

"Are you happy?" I asked her for the first time.

"Yes I am. You are happy now. I am happy."

And for the first time I saw that she could just be fulfilled with a grown-up daughter, a steady job, good food and good friends. I could be happy too with an income and a boyfriend, even without drugs.

She was still my mother, whether she was a spy or not.

I still had not managed to sort out whether I had suffered from paranoid delusions from empathy or not. It would only upset her and Truong if I asked and might cause me another visit to the hospital. So I kept my observations to myself.

And if empathy made the world a more peaceful place, then so be it.

Just because their compassion was caused by empathy didn't make the peaceful decisions of the UN less real.

They did not need to know the truth.

It was enough for me to get by for now.

Hanoi – Vuong

The next morning Giang and Khanh did not hide their unease going to see Lien.

"She's not crazy," I reassured them but I could not hide my doubt. "She's not crazy-violent," I amended.

- We don't want her in our heads.
- You don't have to. Just picture a wall… Yes, like that. I can't see you. There's nothing to be afraid of.

We caught the train and Evelyn met with us on the platform for the Department.

Giang and Khanh presented, as they always did, like a pair of two friendly cats, greeting her civilly. They stayed aloof from my resentment, which I could not hide and they could not totally erase.

I was painfully aware that without their influence I would be furious, maybe even violently angry, at Evelyn and the Department for messing with my life.

Instead, I was left with simmering resentment like teenage rebellion.

Khanh and Giang did not disguise their gratitude. They thought that CHESS and the Department were being co-operative with their wishes. I did not disabuse them of that, merely noting that they had been holding us apart for twenty years.

Khanh and Giang grew quieter and more anxious as we entered the detention centre. They had never been in a Departmental facility as adults and they were remembering when we were separated at five.

They now remembered the Department, CHESS and their true power.

"How is Lien?" I asked Evelyn as we were searched on the way in.

"She's much better. Since she saw you, she's been functioning a lot better. She's even started talking to others. Been more human."

When we reached the door of her room, I found myself holding my breath like Khanh and Giang. I held their hands as Evelyn swiped us in.

Lien looked up. She looked different somehow and I realised what it was. She was smiling.

She leapt into telepathy like a fish to water.

- I have been waiting for you. Ever since Vuong came. Thank you Vuong for bringing them.

I was embarrassed. I had done nothing much to ensure the visit. Except being a good multiple.

- We need to talk aloud. We need to hide the telepathy, Giang reminded us.

"I'm so happy to see you three," Lien gushed. "Even if I don't get to see Geraldine this is just as good. How is Geraldine?"

"She's... strong," I said, looking at Khanh and Giang. They were afraid of feeling what Geraldine was feeling being terminally ill. I was beginning to get impatient with their cowardice and I could not hide it.

"How are you?" Khanh asked.

"I'm happy now you are here," Lien said. "They said if we all co-operate and do their tests we'll get to live together in the CHESS compound. Wouldn't that be good?"

- Emotional blackmail, Khanh commented. *We don't want her to live in detention.*

My entire life I've been manipulated, I thought – the fact of Camille made me feel exploited. That Lien was being used against me by the Department to get what they wanted was just another trick.

"It would be good to live together," Giang said. "We were doing tests in New Zealand so it's no different doing them in Hanoi. But we still want freedom of movement and to still reside in Auckland some of the time."

"You would live in Hanoi?" I asked her, astonished.

"Ever since we knew that we had sisters in Hanoi we have thought about being reunited this way," Khanh said. "We have to tidy up some things in Auckland but our work is done over the internet so we can be anywhere."

- You can choose to go along with what they propose or not. We choose to go along because it suits us for now. We want to keep an eye out for the development of empathy and we can do this best from the inside.

- I see... I agree.

For the first time since my knowledge of Camille's betrayal I felt some hope that things could work out for we.

"I'd like us to live together," I said, for Evelyn's benefit. "I'll take responsibility for you, Lien."

Lien smiled and her happiness infected the three of us like empathy.

Awash with good feeling, I felt euphoric.

We were we.

I felt better than my common sense told me I should feel.

Then I realised I was feeling what the others were feeling a thousandfold. Their joy at being reunited and the prospect of being together overruled everything else.

I was swamped with good will.

- *I have dreamt of you,* Lien thought.
- *We know. We have dreamt of you too*, said Giang.
- *There is nothing to be angry at anymore*, Khanh said.
- *Except Camille,* I found myself broadcasting, unwittingly.

I felt the mental equivalent of a caress and then the physical comfort of the other three women as we embraced each other in a group hug. My resentment was erased again, washed away like a bad dream.

"How is it here?" Khanh asked aloud.

"What you'd expect," Lien said, abiding by our caution to not let others know of our telepathy.

"They have told me that my brain chemistry has changed over the past few weeks since Vuong has visited. I've grown in empathy for humans and I resemble a normal person more – or what passes for normal." Lien laughed as she admitted it.

We shared with her the research that had been done with us since we'd been born and the design of empathy. Strangely she was all in favour of empathy being released into the water supply.

"After you have seen some of the people in here, you would not be able to get empathy in them quickly enough," she said aloud.

We were unable to contradict her. We could feel her fear of some of the other prisoners in her head.

- People need to know about the Department using empathy, Khanh insisted.
- To what end? Lien asked. *What would they do? Overthrow the Department?*

Khanh was silent, but it was obvious what she thought.

- If more people felt empathy for animals the world would turn vegetarian. That can't be a bad thing, Lien suggested.
- We'll go public and let the majority decide, Giang said.
- If that makes you happy, Lien acquiesced. *I don't have anything to lose. But Vuong might.*

I was the only one with reservations about going to the media. I might not be employable again if I was linked to conspiracy theories.

I was touched that Lien had thought of my interests.

I was suspicious at how easy it was for Giang and Khanh to get their way with we. There were two of them, and only one each of me and Lien. Even if Lien and I agreed with each other we couldn't go up against the twins easily. We weren't used to thinking together in concert. The telepathy only worked when both the twins were present. It was a limited gift, a limited blessing.

If an entire population was compliant with empathy, the majority would get their way, suggested Giang and Khanh.

- Like the atmosphere at a music concert or a festival gathering, I suggested.
- Or a demonstration, Khanh and Giang added.

- *Would it be for peace? I hope so.*

- *We can only try*, Khanh thought.

- *To do what is right*, suggested Giang.

- *I agree about exposing the Department's use of empathy at least.* Whether we came out to the world as clones was another thing all together.

- *Yes,* agreed Lien and I felt her smile magnified through we.

I felt better about it then, though I doubted where my sense of wellbeing came from. Giang and Khanh reached out to me and I embraced them back. I could not stay resenting them for long, and they knew that. But then I felt Lien's genuine happiness at being with we and I was reminded of the gift we shared.

- *We are we – no matter what came between us in the past, we can now let go in the present,* Khanh thought.

I agreed.

Berlin – My

There was a terrorist attack at Alexanderplatz. At least that was the first report when a car drove onto the U-Bahn tracks and hit six people. Later it was revealed that the driver thought he was being persecuted for being a member of Islamic State and that Allah was telling him to kill. He was delusional, with a history of mental illness, and IS disclaimed responsibility.

When I read the news, I felt a blow to the stomach. It could have been me waiting at the U-Bahn stop. I bought flowers, purple orchids, and laid them down at the spot where the six people had died. The pile of bouquets stretched out beyond the tram tracks.

I wondered whether empathy could have prevented this from happening.

Truong wanted to go to Drei regardless.

"If there is such a thing as a saturation point it is worth a lot of euro," he explained to me as he filled up his backpack.

I decided to accompany him. I felt some sense of responsibility for what would happen. The higher-grade empathy had just been delivered and I was curious as to what it would be like, conspiracy or no conspiracy.

Berghain was thumping when we got there. Somehow word had got out that Truong had superior product – he was bailed up as soon as he got in the queue.

I stood next to him, my arms crossed. He had not offered any to me and I wondered whether he thought I was still drug-affected like Freja and my mother thought I was.

We entered the club and made our way to the couches on the second floor. Soon Truong ran out of product to sell.

He had one pack left and finally he offered some to me, putting out his hand.

"Try it," he suggested.

I held the tablet in my hand.

"Here's to peace," he said swallowing his own. He smiled and leant back on the couch. "Saturation point. Mission accomplished."

I looked at him, an ugly suspicion growing in my mind. Suddenly I remembered things again, words not said, silences with different meanings. My memories started making sense. It all clicked into place.

"It's you! You're being paid by the North!"

His smile did not falter, though his eyes told a different story.

"All this time I've suspected my mother and it was you all along!"

He did not try to deny it. He let my accusation do the talking for him.

"Does it matter where my money comes from?" he asked softly. "It's all in the name of peace. We get the South Sea back, we're one step closer to peace in the Middle East and we may prevent countless would-be terrorist attacks. Even the local neo-Nazis are placated with empathy. If we just prevent one massacre, isn't it worth it?"

His worldview was so seductive he had me almost believing it.

"What about free will? People aren't choosing to have peace..." I protested.

"What is free will? Do we honestly have free will when we live in a society influenced by others? Empathy just amplifies what is there."

I thought about what had happened to me in Việt Nam and felt sick in the stomach.

"People choose to take empathy," he continued. "They know of the risks."

I was stunned mute. It was as if he was disclaiming responsibility.

"Make your choice, My. You know all the facts now."

I stared at him, astounded at his duplicity.

"You just used me to get information about CHESS," I said. I was so hurt.

"No, I didn't, My. That was a hallucination. Freja was right. I didn't use you. I like you."

I felt another gaping hole in my recollections. It was disconcerting for a moment. Then a sense of wellbeing intruded upon me, the effect of empathy.

"My funders just want peace. They want to stop China's dominance and aggression in the long term. Creating peace in the Western world to unite is one way of doing this. It's a good thing, My. What I'm doing is for the common good. It's good for trade."

"You keep telling yourself that," I muttered. His justifications seemed paper-thin to me. I remembered being used as a mule. If I had known, would I have done it?

The Vietnamese government had the black market under its control with Truong, I realised.

I had pulled myself up short.

I didn't know.

"I don't blame you if you don't want to see me anymore," he said.

His genuine sorrow made me almost want to forgive him. But he had let me think my understanding was just a conspiracy theory and that my mother was ex-Stasi. That, I could not forgive. I could not trust a thing he said.

"You're right. I don't want to see you anymore," I said, knowing I'd regret it.

"Okay. It was nice knowing you, My Nguyen," he said, formally.

He leant in for a kiss and I moved away in disgust.

The bass beats rang in my ears as he picked up his backpack and walked into the crowd of dancers.

I tried not to regret it as tears built up in my eyes only to be swept away by a feeling of calm.

Damned empathy.

I was as emotional as a junkie coming down.

I looked at the tablet in my hand. A desire for the drug took me then, to obliterate the complex of emotions I had. Furious, I stopped myself, closing my hand into a fist.

Truong was not who I had thought he had been. The man I had thought I loved wasn't real.

He had manipulated me into doing what he wanted for the Vietnamese government.

I felt dirty then. I would have preferred it if he had been just a selfish drug dealer as I had thought. Then I would have known where I stood.

Out on the dance floor I saw Freja and Mattias dancing. They were wreathed in smiles, and I knew that, all unknowing, they were part of the saturation point.

Everyone was part of the saturation point. I saw it all then, the network of drug dealers, multi-national pharmaceutical companies, the hui circles behind the scenes, and the scheming of governments to engineer peace. From domestic neo-Nazi hatred to the rivalry of nations.

It was big, enormous, beyond comprehension. And no one would believe me if I tried to tell them. And if I did, who would condemn it?

It wasn't killing anybody. At least not yet, as I understood it. Even if I outed Truong, it would achieve nothing. The saturation point had been reached, the effect would self-perpetuate.

Nothing could stop it.

I felt peace settle on me then, replacing the anger I had towards Truong. I couldn't stay angry in the atmosphere of the club. The saturation point was so effective… However it might have been achieved, it created peace…

I could just enjoy it, keeping the knowledge of the bigger picture to myself…

I opened my hand again. My sweat made the tablet melt a little on my palm, smearing it pink.

What was the right thing to do?

Freja had been correct about my thoughts of my mother as ex-Stasi being delusional. I owed her an apology. And my mother too.

Would they believe me if I told them about Truong?

Did it matter?

Apart from my wounded pride, did it make a difference?

I joined Freja on the dance floor. She embraced me and Mattias and I felt their acceptance and love. And I loved them back.

Freja's platonic friendship and love was real. I had always known that. As much as I now knew that my mother loved me and wanted my happiness.

I did not need empathy to tell me what was true. Or what to feel.

I crumbled the empathy tablet in my hand and emptied the remains onto the dance floor.

I have made my choice.

Sydney – Vuong

Going back to Sydney with the twins, their reluctance to see Geraldine dragged on me like a lead anchor. I tried to show them how Geraldine was, a sad picture in my mind, nothing to be afraid of. I knew that they were coming along to humour me – my disappointment upset them and cut them to the core.

The reunion would be like meeting Lien. It was only this comparison that got them to agree to come along.

We arrived at the respite house and clambered out of the cab. The driver said nothing, just pocketed his fare and left us.

The same nurse was on duty and did a double take in greeting Khanh and Giang.

"Your sisters look alike, Geraldine," she said.

Geraldine nodded. She was thinner than I remembered, but her eyes still shone brightly and sharpened up when she saw Khanh and Giang. Khanh and Giang took in a deep breath when they made eye contact and I felt the shock to their systems. There was an echo of Geraldine's weakness in her body, and an ache from her back. She was dying and fragile as an insect.

But Khanh and Giang did not die. They took another breath and stood a distance away. They erected a wall between them and Geraldine and me.

I mirrored them and concentrated on the sensations in my body, grounding myself in my senses away from the others.

I was healthy and sound of mind. The feelings of the others were on my periphery now.

"Hello girls," Geraldine said, greeting us with a smile.

- *Hello,* said Khanh.

"Hello, Geraldine," said Giang.

- *You are speaking in my head,* Geraldine observed.
- *Yes,* said Khanh.

"I'd prefer it if you didn't do that," Geraldine said.

- *Okay.*

"I mean, okay," said Khanh, shocked. "But why?"

Geraldine looked at me and then at the twins.

"I've been independent for a long time. Now that I am dying, I want the privacy of my own mind. Don't get me wrong, I'm happy to see the two of you. But I can also feel your fear of my death and I don't need that."

Mortified, Khanh and Giang looked at each other.

"We're sorry," they both said together and held hands. I felt them raise a wall again, a stronger one, between them and me and Geraldine. I caught a sense of pity for Geraldine and then nothing.

Then Giang offered her other hand to Geraldine. Geraldine accepted it and held out her hand to me. I accepted the simple comfort and squeezed it.

"By the way, thank you for coming. I wish Lien could have come but our government would not have given her a visa. It is good to see you."

Geraldine's inclusive smile made up for all the previous complications. I relaxed into the simple company of we.

"I'm glad that you are all staying together in Hanoi for a while. I wish I could join you." Tears glimmered in her eyes and I squeezed her hand hard.

"But with all their tests, have you found what it is that they are looking for?" she asked Giang.

"It's to make a better grade of empathy," Giang divulged cautiously.

"Did you know there is a conspiracy theory that empathy is being put in drinking water to make people peaceful?" Geraldine said. "I heard it's through the clubbing scene that empathy is pacifying the Berlin population," Geraldine continued quietly. "They say it's reaching a critical mass. A saturation point."

I exchanged glances with the twins. Geraldine was discussing openly and freely what was being kept secret in Việt Nam and among ourselves.

- We are unmonitored, supposedly, Khanh commented.
- Can we trust this and talk aloud?
- Geraldine does.

"It's not just a conspiracy theory," I told her. "It's possible."

Geraldine laughed.

"I don't think so," she replied.

"Well, is it just a conspiracy theory that five clones have been created that the world thinks are quintuplets, that are being used for tests to develop empathy?" Giang suggested.

"Point taken," Geraldine replied.

"What you say is true in Việt Nam. Doing it in Berlin, though…"

"They are doing it in Việt Nam?" Geraldine's eyes sharpened, thinking. She was not surprised. "After the Wall fell there were still ex-Stasi around from East Berlin. They may have links to the Vietnamese government, it's not totally out of the question," she remarked.

We thought about this for a moment and digested this.

The four of us shared a group hug. I missed the telepathy but still felt the empathic response of the twins to Geraldine. I think she felt it too once they had gotten over their fear. I felt closeness and wellbeing wash over we.

We are we.

We went to Auckland for a few weeks for the twins to arrange their move. I spent the time being a tourist, trying to forget about Camille. It was like Ma had always said. The only people I could trust were my sisters. Every time I thought of Camille it was to remember her betrayal. Everything I had felt for her had been built on a lie. She knew more about me than I did. I had worried about hiding things from her, while she had been deceiving me all along.

The others wanted to be strategic in revealing the truth about the development of empathy. We needed Lien out of detention and set up in Hanoi as a resident like us. And we needed to meet My Nguyen, the author of the saturation point paper, and see if she was for real.

Khanh and Giang could only influence my mood so much. When I was alone my feelings of resentment and anger came back. The Department was running my life again.

It was okay for Khanh and Giang. They were used to only relying on each other. Or so I thought. But when we four would move in together in Hanoi and I would see Lien's face giddy with happiness and freedom, it would make it all worthwhile.

Hanoi – Vuong

Geraldine passed away suddenly.

We all woke up that night at the same time of her passing. We gathered in the kitchen and waited for the official notification by phone.

Khanh and Giang felt guilty about their unwarranted fear. Her death was a sudden sense of something missing. A winking out of light. A feeling of absence.

There was no threat to our sense of being.

We murmured the Buddhist Heart Sutra together.

Form is emptiness, emptiness is form. Gone, gone to the other shore.

We had a Buddhist memorial service in Hanoi at the local temple for her attended just by we. We did not know whether Ma had a family plot or any plans for us when we died. But we knew that the Department would have examined her body in Australia before burying her.

We held hands together in a circle. We shared ourselves in grief and the sadness was tinged with gratitude that we were able to see her before she died.

- *I wish she was not scared of this*, Giang said.
- *I understand why*, I said.
- *It's what makes us different*, Khanh observed.

- *Not necessarily a bad thing,* I commented.

- *I'm glad we are we,* Lien said soberly. *I wish I could have met Geraldine. She feels hard in your minds. Maybe I could have made her less afraid.*

I thought of nothing then and maintained my wall. It was becoming automatic for me now to project my thoughts when I wanted to, and to always have my wall in the background of my consciousness when around the twins. They respected that and I liked them the more for it.

I wondered what effect empathy would have on their telepathy but veered away from wanting to know. I only had my experience of empathy with Camille to draw on, and even that was tainted with my knowledge of her spying on me.

It was that which made me realise that her feelings for me were real – at least her attraction to me was real, amplified by empathy. Empathy could not pick up cognition, at least not with the batches that were being produced now. I wondered whether refining the drug using the data from us multiples would result in telepathy. And whether it would be a desired outcome.

- *That's why we need to keep it secret,* Khanh murmured into my thoughts.

- *They would use us if they knew what we could do.*

- *If everyone could feel and think as we do it might be okay,* said Lien. *I'm not angry anymore and it's because of you two.*

- People might respond in fear like Geraldine, Khanh replied.
It may not be a good outcome. Fear and anger can spread
like wildfire.
- What if empathy was being seeded in Berlin during the
Drei festival? Apparently it had no arrests and nothing
untoward was reported. In the UN Security Council meet-
ing in Berlin at the same time China seceded the South
Sea to Việt Nam without aggression. If this was the result
of empathy as the conspiracy theorists say, then it is a
good thing.
- Do you believe it?
- The originator of that theory is Vietnamese-German. My
Nguyen. I've checked her social media presence. She's an
undergraduate student at Humboldt doing an arts degree.
Pretty ordinary otherwise.
- Maybe we should meet her now. Find out if this is
the truth.
- And if it is, what then?

There was silence.

- We can work them from the inside, Khanh suggested.
They want us to co-operate with their tests to develop
empathy. We can manipulate results. Conduct industrial
espionage and sabotage. When the time is right.

The anger I felt at the Department channelled into cold
thinking at what we could do. Even just the data I had seen
of the tests on the five of us was worth millions in possible
genome development.

- We are we. And they will not have total control over us ever again, Khanh vowed.

And we agreed.

We had gotten used to being a foursome before we underwent our first tests for the Department. Evelyn accompanied we. I felt an absurd gratitude towards her, for her being instrumental in we being reunited. Her good word to the Department had helped us gain access.

We went to the Department building that I was familiar with, where I had had my previous bloodwork and tests done. I could feel the trepidation of the twins and Lien's nervousness.

- It's okay, I tried to reassure them, even though I was worried myself.
- You've been here before, Khanh said.
- Yes. They run tests here.

We arrived at a large medical consulting room. We were instructed to roll up our sleeves and be ready for blood tests. We were administered two at a time. It all seemed perfectly legitimate.

But then they told us they were running a blind trial of a vaccine on us.

"We didn't sign up for that!" Khanh protested as they readied the dose.

"You are needed for the trial," Evelyn said.

"I refuse," Khanh said.

"You can if you wish. But then we will place Lien and Vuong in detention. They will be forced to participate in the trial. It's better if you volunteer now."

I was aghast. I saw a side to Evelyn I'd never seen before.

But I was not surprised by the threat. Neither was Lien.

Khanh looked at both of us.

"I will tell the New Zealand government that we were forced under duress to be part of the trial."

"You can do that," Evelyn said dismissively, and that comment made me more afraid. "We have a research agreement with New Zealand. This is legitimate."

- We could force our way out, but they'd detain us.
- Co-operate for now. We'll think of a way to escape later.

Khanh and Giang reluctantly agreed to the injection first. Then me and Lien received the jab.

We were accompanied by Evelyn on the return to our house.

She left us then, to my relief. My anger at her almost eclipsed the anger I still had for Camille.

- Where can we escape to?

We sat around the kitchen table having tea. We suspected the house was bugged so kept our conversation going in our heads.

- We could go to Berlin. They wouldn't expect us to go there. We can meet My and find out more about the saturation point and empathy, I suggested.

The others considered this.

- I know of someone who can make fake identity papers, Lien volunteered.
- So we just need to get to the airport. We can go separately in twos and meet there. It looks less suspicious than all four of us travelling together.

I smiled at our plan.

Lien got the fake papers and I booked our flights online. The twins volunteered to split up, realising that Lien had not flown before.

We reached the airport without incident.

I was nervous at immigration and let Giang take the lead. The airport was large and sterile. The immigration officer was bored and barely glanced at our passports.

We sat away from each other and my anxiety grew as we waited for the gates to open.

I stood up at the boarding announcement and Giang put her hand on my shoulder.

"Relax. There's plenty of time."

They checked our passports and tickets again to move us into a different lounge.

I sat down, chafing.

Giang held my hand and a sense of calm washed over me.

"Khanh and Lien are doing fine," she told me. I restrained myself from looking for them, instead focusing on Giang, who seemed totally relaxed with the airport procedures.

The final call came over the PA and we were herded onto the bus that took us to the aircraft. I tried to emulate the other passengers, resigned and patient.

Taking my seat, wedged between the window and Giang, I felt a sudden panic.

She held my hand tightly and I tried a small smile for her. The air was thin and sterile.

The announcements came in German and Vietnamese and I felt a sense of jarring. I was going to a foreign country. In a plane.

Leaving Việt Nam, perhaps forever.

I was pressed back into my seat as the plane took off.

It was easy – too easy.

We should have realised that.

Berlin – My

The first I heard of the multiples was when they contacted me after reading my article linked to a fake news site. I was suspicious, and doubly so when they claimed to be clones used to test empathy. Their article about multi-nationals like CHESS using clones to test new drugs like empathy was linked to mine by content. People who were interested in the saturation point also read about cloning. And about dating twins.

It was so wild that there had to be a grain of truth to it, I guessed. They were coming to Berlin and wanted to meet me. I told Freja about it, in case something happened to me. She met my proposition with disbelief but agreed to check in with me every hour on the hour.

I named a popular café in Kreuzberg. They were easy to spot, four similar-looking Asian women in jeans and jumpers sitting closely together.

Four of them and one of me. I felt surrounded, then one of them held out her hand for me to shake.

"Giang," she said, and I felt the warmth of her smile and their welcome. The foursome were dressed in different-coloured tops. That was the only thing that really set them apart – their short hairstyles were not that different.

"My," I said and sat down at the table. We ordered coffee and cake and I felt their closeness. Seeing them, I could believe that they were the clones they claimed to be.

"I appreciate you meeting with me," I said. "It means a lot to me that at least someone believes me." I spoke in Vietnamese, highly conscious of my German accent.

"We know what it's like to not be believed," Khanh said.

"What we are interested in is what you intend to do with the knowledge you have," said Vuong boldly. "CHESS intends to patent all its findings and lock up its discoveries for twenty years before needing to share them in the public domain. We are in a position to leak information about what they are doing now that we are out of Hanoi."

The clones had told me of their tests at CHESS when they had first contacted me after reading the article I had written about empathy. The lone genuine engagement with my article. Their story seemed even more improbable than mine. Even I doubted it at first. Seeing them was literally believing.

"We could claim our test data as being ours if it came down to it," Giang suggested.

"CHESS would claim ownership. But once it's released, its advantages in secrecy have gone." Khanh was straight to the point and direct in Vietnamese.

"They will discredit whatever we release," Khanh continued. "But if the material is circulated for long enough and people become familiar enough with it they will be less shocked and more inclined to believe in more unlikely-seeming claims."

I blinked. The women had clearly thought about this over time.

"We also need to think about where we want the information about empathy development to originate from," Giang added. "We could have the information originating in Việt Nam and confirmed by a source in Berlin with you and your contacts. And then we can confirm from Auckland, making it global."

The others nodded, smiling. My initial unease was replaced by a sense of wellbeing. We were doing the right thing. What they were suggesting made sense.

"I'll do a mini-documentary about you on my phone and put it on YouTube," I suggested. "Hopefully it will go viral."

"Even if it doesn't it still will be out there for people to find if they look for it," Vuong said.

I smiled and the clones nodded to me.

"With you verifying the information about empathy it will be more credible. And we can drip-feed the information about your cloning," I suggested.

The women nodded again like a chorus, disconcerting me a little. But their friendliness made me feel like I could trust them. Like a low dose of empathy.

"I'll confirm your information from here," I promised. "We can do it in English, German and Vietnamese."

I felt the tightness in my chest loosen at their agreement. For the first time since Truong's admission, I felt like I was in control of my life again.

"People will do what they want with the information. If they choose not to believe, we have at least tried," Khanh said dismissively. "And if we go public the Department will be subject to outside scrutiny. It would not be able to keep how it treats us a secret."

They wanted to share the information and data sets collected from them with the world. And their knowledge of empathy. I understood their altruism and I could help them.

It made what I had experienced worthwhile. Almost.

I could trust again even after Truong, I thought as I watched the clones finish their coffee and cake.

There was a companiable silence as we ate. Then it seemed as if by an unspoken signal the four women turned towards me to confide in me.

"We had to leave Hanoi in a hurry," Khanh said sotto voce. "Are there many Vietnamese in Berlin?"

"There are a few..." I said vaguely. I did not know what "many" would mean to them. Hanoi was more than "a few."

"There are Vietnamese restaurants and a market," I told them.

"Could you help us find a place to stay?" she asked.

"Like an apartment? Or a house to live in?"

"A house."

I felt pinned down by the stare of the multiples. The least I could do was help them find accommodation in Berlin. I found myself wanting to help them. It seemed the least I could do for people who believed in me.

It did not occur to me at the time that my feeling of good will towards them was generated by the multiples' presence and charisma.

I was more horrified at the thought of people being used like lab rats.

"I can find a house for you," I offered. "Are you planning to stay long?"

The multiples exchanged glances.

"A few weeks at first," Khanh said. "We will see if Berlin is a good place for us. Me and Giang can work anywhere. But Lien and Vuong are different. We have to see if our company can employ them."

"I'll see what I can do," I replied. A sense of wellbeing engulfed me when they smiled, not unlike the contentment I had post-empathy.

I frowned and Giang looked at me quizzically.

"Is there something wrong?" Giang asked me.

"No, nothing. I just think it's incredible what they have done with empathy. With you girls. Have you tried empathy?"

Vuong nodded. Khanh, Lien and Giang shook their heads in unison.

"Do you believe in the saturation point?"

"It's believable," said Lien. "In Việt Nam its believable. But in Berlin... You have people demonstrating against vaccines! That's the opposite of what empathy is about!"

"Yes," I said, ashamed of being German in that instance.

"Individualist cultures do worse and are less compliant with public health directions," Vuong said. "Look at the USA. Thousands of deaths to the flu. All preventable by vaccines."

"Berlin could be worse," I muttered.

At least we were in a democracy, I thought.

Berlin – Vuong

Berlin seemed empty for a capital city. I was doubly grateful we had My for a guide. She had found an Airbnb for us to stay in, in Kreuzberg. The cooler air was my first impression of Berlin, and then the mix of people – we were in a Turkish neighbourhood which also had a Vietnamese restaurant where My worked. Germans were not all white, blonde and blue-eyed.

My was a pretty girl with a pert, welcoming smile.

And only a scattering of people wore masks.

This surprised we. Why wouldn't you wear masks to stop the flu viruses?

"Do Germans want to die?" Lien asked My.

My shrugged. She was wearing a mask outside, as were the four of we.

"Women don't wear masks in Berlin to protect their skin from the sun and dirt like women in Việt Nam. We're not used to wearing masks," My explained.

Lien saw everything with wonder, she had never been out of Hanoi.

Most of the people lived in apartments in central Berlin, but we were fortunate enough to find a large house with four bedrooms.

When we arrived at the house and put down our bags, I felt freed at last. The feeling was mutual for all of us. Lien and I in particular had escaped possible detention – the twins had not felt threatened in the same way, being citizens of New Zealand.

We seemed to have gotten away. It was easy, too easy, and I could not help but suspect we had been let go, rather than escaping of our own volition.

I could not help but wonder whether Camille would know where I had gone. It was a relief to be somewhere she had never been, where I had no memories of her.

We sat in the lounge after eating pho at My's restaurant. It was too sweet with MSG, but we were polite and ate it without comment.

Khanh and Giang were busy finding the research protocols concerning us by hacking into the Departmental servers. We wanted to know our bloodwork and what possible consequences were for our health.

"We've found it," Khanh said. "They were testing the latest novel flu vaccine on us."

It was what the world needed. And we had just sabotaged it.

"Well, what can we do? We can't go back!" Khanh exclaimed.

"According to the protocol the next bloodwork is in three days. We could get the samples ourselves and send them back to them…" Giang suggested.

"How?"

"We can ask My. She might know a doctor. She'd also might know of Vietnamese government contacts. Or we could contact the embassy…"

"Not the embassy," I said. "We aren't going back. Nor telling the government we are here. They don't need our samples."

"We can help with the vaccine," Khanh said.

"Not at the expense of our freedom," I said.

"I don't want to go back to detention," Lien protested.

- We'll just find a way to give them our bloodwork. They don't need to know where we are.

Khanh and Giang soothed Lien and tried to sooth me with good will. I struggled to hold on to my anger.

"You are New Zealand citizens. You do not run the same risk as me and Lien."

"We'll just ask My. There's no harm in that."

We called My and she came over with some banh mi.

We told her of our dilemma, and she fell quiet, thinking.

"The world needs more vaccines. I know someone who has contacts with the Vietnamese government. He could help." She swallowed and looked up at me.

"I don't want to talk to him. But this is important. Are you sure this is what you want?"

"We have to try," Giang said. "We are a special set for research. We have to think of the greater good. It was why we were created, after all."

I stared at Giang. She actually still believed in the rationale the Department had brought us up on.

"We can help the world," Giang continued, sensing my dismay. "It's our purpose."

I felt Khanh's agreement. Lien was surprised and confused. She withdrew behind a wall. I did the same. I wanted to be alone with my own thoughts to make my own decision, free of the twins' influence.

I did not want to be part of a blind group mind. Not with my life at stake.

BERLIN – MY

I did not want to see Truong again. But he was the way into the Vietnamese government. I didn't know if he would give the clones away to be put in detention but that was a risk they wanted to take.

Telling them about Truong, I felt anew how he had used me. Vuong held my hand, and I could feel their sympathy.

"It sounds like the Department to me," Vuong said. "They used someone I loved against me too."

She told me the story of Camille and I was touched by her sharing the intimate details with me. I squeezed her small, warm hand in consolation.

"And that's why we should not go back," Vuong concluded. "They will just use us and imprison us. They will detain me and Lien at the very least and if they are bold they'll get Khanh and Giang too."

"If they use our blood, it will be on our terms," Khanh said. "Two of us will go with you, My. This Truong can be a courier between us. We'll deal with him directly after you introduce us, you don't need to be involved."

"It's okay," I replied, even though I knew it wouldn't be. I would still want to know. I would feel responsible for what would happen to them.

"We still shouldn't do this," Lien said. "There are other people being used in clinical trials. What is one data set to them? We are only four samples and they need hundreds to prove safety…"

"We are a special set being multiple and you know that," Khanh said.

"They won't dare do anything to us if we have My along as a German witness," Giang argued. I opened my mouth, then shut it again.

"I know that you're scared. I don't blame you. We'll get the doctor to take the blood samples at a place of our choosing. You won't see anyone from the government," Khanh reassured them.

"You're being naive if you think we can just give blood samples and they'll leave us alone," Vuong said.

"We can threaten to harm ourselves and sabotage their findings," Khanh declared, and I felt the shock of Vuong and Lien at how far Khanh and Giang were prepared to go.

"Only as a last measure," Giang said, and I felt her trying to smooth things over for the other two. "We want to do this for the good of other people. Practise true empathy. We can be truly altruistic. We do run a risk, yes, but right now we can stay in Berlin and with My's assistance we can help the world."

I kept my mouth shut. The talk about vaccines had me out of my depth. I understood Vuong's and Lien's fears. Truong was deceptive and I could not guarantee them anything. But the twins still wanted to risk it and I respected that.

"You two can do what you like. But we'll stay out of it," Vuong said.

Khanh and Giang ended up accompanying me to Truong's flat. They wanted to see his initial reaction to them not mediated by a phone or the internet.

I was not surprised. I suspected I was feeling more, possibly still influenced by empathy. I felt a special closeness to Vuong, holding her hand after hearing about Camille.

My heart started racing as we got off the U-Bahn and headed to Truong's flat. I found myself nervous, and I hated feeling this way.

Khanh glanced at me and squeezed my hand.

I felt a kinship with her and Giang too, like empathy. I did not stop to wonder if it was real or a consequence of empathy. The net effect was the same.

I banged on the door to Truong's flat.

There was silence.

Khanh and Giang looked at me. It was eleven. In the morning.

"Maybe he's out…" I speculated and then the door opened.

His hair was in spikes and he wore a T-shirt and tracksuit pants, awoken from sleep. I still felt an echo of my attraction to him, and I hated it.

"My... Guten Morgen. And..."

"Khanh and Giang," Khanh said. "We have some business for you." She spoke in Vietnamese.

"Come in. Excuse the mess," Truong said after a moment.

We sat down on his couch. The mess looked the same as when I had last crashed there.

"Your other sisters are not here," Truong said, speaking Vietnamese, and Khanh looked at me in surprise. "I know who you are, or more like what you are. I've been told to look for you. You are like your picture."

"You are working for the Vietnamese government," Khanh stated.

"Yes. She knows." He indicated me. "I'm surprised you're here. How are you?"

I looked at him, astounded that he would ask.

"I'm okay. And you?"

"Busy. I've been told to find you." He turned to Khanh again. "You are..."

"I'm Khanh. But don't you already know that?"

Khanh was on the defensive and I willed her not to be.

"I'm Truong. The government pays me for services rendered. Such as locating people. But I'm not about to turn you in. We're in Berlin, a democracy. Hanoi does not have that power in Germany. They can observe but not interfere. You and your sister are from New Zealand, at any rate."

"We want to liaise with someone who can reach the health department in Hanoi. We were part of vaccine research for influenza, and we wish to continue the bloodwork but in Berlin. As free agents."

"Ah," Truong said and I could see his mind ticking over.

"CHESS has the necessary equipment," I said. "And they have a Hanoi subsidiary."

"And you want payment yourselves?"

"We wish to be left alone," Khanh said. "We will do the bloodwork for the greater good. In exchange for our freedom."

Truong nodded then looked at me.

"I'll talk to my contacts. How shall I get in contact with you?"

"Contact me," I said. There was no need for him to have the details of the multiples.

"How did you get involved with this?" he asked me.

"They contacted me about the saturation point," I told him reluctantly. I didn't want him to know anything about me anymore.

"It is good of you to do the bloodwork. You risk everything coming to me." Khanh smiled in acknowledgement. I, on the other hand, stifled an urge to slap him out of his smugness. "I'll be in touch, My," he said in parting, showing us the door.

Berlin – Vuong

We enjoyed the freedom of Berlin. Compared to Hanoi it was quiet and orderly. We were unusual, a group of Asian women in masks, and sometimes drew more attention than warranted. The askance looks we got made me think Germans did not see Asians very often.

The centre of Berlin was marked by where the Berlin Wall used to be. Checkpoint Charlie was a tourist spot. The dead were commemorated with bronze plaques in the pavement outside where they had once lived. Their World War II history was a constant landmarked reminder, like the Vietnamese/American War memorials in Hanoi.

We didn't know what to expect. We had withdrawn a large amount of American dollars before we left Hanoi, but things were expensive here. Khanh and Giang still worked online and they generously shared their salaries with we. They also tried to line up work for me and Lien with their company. They were hopeful for me being a researcher but less hopeful for Lien, who had not gone to university.

I could not stay angry at Khanh and Giang for long. When they returned from meeting with Truong it was as if nothing had happened. We fit together like a pair of gloves. They described a smart, handsome young man who was not a threat at all. And they came back with a supply of empathy.

Watching the news and the death toll of the latest strain of influenza, I began to wonder whether I had made a mistake. People were dying.

I asked Lien out for coffee away from Khanh and Giang.

"I'm thinking of changing my mind about giving my blood sample," I said to her as soon as we were out of the house.

Lien smiled suddenly and I realised she had been thinking along the same lines as well.

"Being test subjects was what Ma made us for," I admitted to Lien. "If we can help CHESS develop a vaccine it is worth it…"

Lien nodded.

We set up a shrine in the house for Geraldine. My took us to the Dong Ma complex and the crowded stalls of mixed goods like the markets in Việt Nam gave me pangs for home. Setting up the shrine with all the accoutrements, white and red flowers, fruits of five different colours and red candles, the smell of incense made me want to cry even more.

We were in exile and might never come home…

I was the only one to feel homesick. But Lien was free and I could not begrudge her that.

Khanh and Giang were quite pragmatic as they assembled the five fruits with their different colours. Apple, oranges, grapes, grapefruits and plums. My took me to a place where I could print out a digital photo of Geraldine. My was spending a lot of time with us. She was a university student and had all the time in the world, it seemed. I found myself talking to her the most. I was the most normal one, I thought cynically, and could relate to her. We both had been betrayed for empathy. She was cute too, I noticed, her eyes bright like a bird's.

"What was Geraldine like?" she asked me as we headed back to the house from the printing shop.

"Sharp. Cynical. Angry she couldn't see all of us sooner."

"I would be furious if I were in the position you girls are in. I can't imagine what it'd be like," My admitted.

"What are German-Vietnamese like? We have a saying that overseas Vietnamese are mat goc and have lost their roots," I asked, changing the subject.

"I'm not Vietnamese, I say I'm German-Vietnamese. A banana. Yellow on the outside, white on the inside," My quipped.

She smiled and I laughed at the thought.

"Truong may work for the government, but he is mat goc," I said. I had noticed the scaly body of a dragon tattoo peeking out from his neckline.

My snorted at the mention of his name.

"Are you in contact with Camille?" she asked me.

"No. I don't want to see her."

"That's understandable."

We reached the house and I let us in.

I put the framed picture in the centre of the shrine.

Red candles were lit next to white gladioli and My and we passed around incense sticks.

We chanted the Heart Sutra together.

Form is emptiness, emptiness is form…

Berlin – My

I was touched that they included me in their ceremony for the forty-ninth day since the death of Geraldine. After spending seven weeks on earth, now was the time the spirit would go to nirvana.

They bought a CD of Buddhist chants from Dong Ma and as it played it was punctuated by the ringing of bells.

I knelt with them on the floor of the lounge room in front of the shrine and a shiver ran down my spine.

Khanh rang the bell a final time as we got to our feet to bow. Then we placed our incense sticks in the urn in front of us. The picture of Geraldine seemed at ease.

We were silent for a few moments.

The clones looked at each other and held hands in a circle. Vuong gestured for me to join in. I felt a zap of static and gasped.

"You feel her?" Vuong asked me.

"I don't know…" I felt peace like empathy.

"I feel peace," I said aloud.

"She is at peace," Lien said softly.

We formed a group hug and I felt buoyed up by the clones.

It was the best I had felt in days. If the saturation point could engender this there would be no need for fighting.

Tears came to my eyes of their own volition. The clones were crying like gentle rain.

We held each other up. I was the first to break away to catch my breath and compose myself. The others came soon after, unfolding like petals from a flower.

They went into the kitchen, and I followed them. They had made lemongrass beef and vermicelli, not just for the shrine offerings but enough for the five of us to share. Without comment, Lien had tofu instead of beef.

I felt included and a sense of wellbeing equal to that of empathy.

I found myself sitting alone with Vuong in the lounge room.

I could not say with honesty whether my feelings for Truong had been caused by empathy or not. The sense of closeness I felt with the twins was eerily similar. I did not feel alone. What I felt for Vuong was something else...

I looked side-on at Vuong. She was the only clone to wear make-up and it defined her beauty and the curve of her cheekbones.

It seemed only natural that we drew close and kissed.

We are both on rebound, I told myself. I felt myself opening to a new tenderness, different to what I felt for Truong.

I recognised my familiar feeling of falling in love with Vuong. She was not as dominant as Khanh but had a quiet confidence and warm, buzzy energy. She was quick to smile, a sweet smile that was cute and curious.

She was unlike Lien, who had a grim seriousness about her, or the calm ethereal peace of the twins.

Now I knew them, I could readily tell them apart. But in falling for Vuong I found myself feeling mildly attracted to all the clones. I understood enough of my own reactions to be grateful that only Vuong reciprocated. I did not want an orgy on empathy.

Again, I wondered how much of what I felt towards the clones was their chemistry, which was the active ingredient of empathy. I started to doubt whether what I felt for Vuong was true.

She was the first woman that I had kissed.

What I felt with Truong was real enough to hurt.

I didn't want to discover that Vuong was for real at the end of what happened between us.

It would be real for Vuong, I intuited. She was vulnerable after Camille. Something inside me that had closed with Truong opened up to her.

Vuong was solid to touch and to rely on. I felt protective towards her. She was intelligent and sensitive and deserved better than to be deceived.

Like me.

Berlin – Vuong

Kissing My reminded me I could feel capable of being away from the clones. I felt strong within myself and My was opaque to me – I could not read her mind.

This comforted me, feeling the solidity of the boundaries of my sense of individual self. Our physical intimacy was a gentle sharing and I did not lose myself the way I did in communion with we.

The psychologist-researcher part of me was fascinated at the differences between my closeness to My and to the clones. My's touch erased the lingering sensory memory I had of Camille.

I felt I could trust My even without reading her mind. And I reluctantly admitted to the clones that I wanted to tell her of our telepathy.

- She has been lied to so much, I want her to know.
- If you really think it is necessary, Khanh said.

The twins did not understand intimacy outside of we, I concluded. And Lien had never been in a relationship.

- Do you trust her?
-We've trusted her so far, I replied.

I wanted My to trust me. And that meant sharing our secrets.

I was not just we. But she needed to know where I stopped and we began.

I hoped she would not reject me and my connection to we. But honesty was best, I thought.

Berlin – My

The other clones just seemed to accept me being with Vuong and did not mention anything to me.

I soon discovered why when Vuong told me about their telepathy.

I immediately felt vulnerable. Could they have spied on us when we kissed?

"Can you read each other's minds?" I said aloud in shock.

"Only if we let we," Vuong said. She squeezed my hand. "We just can talk to each other when we can physically see each other. We can block each other out. It can be very limited."

I stared at her and then glared at Giang, who came into the lounge room where we sat.

"Are you talking now?" I asked.

Giang and Vuong answered together.

"Yes."

"How can I know you are not talking behind my back? I mean talking in front of me telepathically?"

"You can't," Giang said. "You have to trust us. You can't prevent us talking literally behind your back anyway."

I was taken aback by her bluntness.

Vuong looked ruefully into my eyes.

"It's a lot to take in, My. Take your time and ask me any questions you have. You are the first person we have confided our telepathy in. We do trust you."

Khanh and Lien came into the room and sat down.

The awkward silence spun out into minutes. I could tell by their postures they were listening to something or someone.

"I don't know how I feel about this," I said. "I will keep it secret. I'm not likely to be believed anyway."

"Thank you," Lien said. The others nodded in a chorus, except Vuong, who chose to kiss me on the cheek.

Another awkward silence fell and I fancied I could see them communing with each other.

It made me angry, I didn't know why.

"I just need some time alone to think about this," I said aloud.

"Okay," said Khanh, and they stood up.

Only Vuong stayed behind as the other clones left the lounge room.

She looked at me sadly.

"I'll be waiting for you," she said and kissed me on the mouth.

My sense of tenderness awoke in me again and I embraced her. This was what I wanted, not the add-on of a telepathic family of clones.

Could I separate my feelings for Vuong from her telepathic link to her clone sisters?

She did not have to tell me, I realised. In the month since we first met, they had been in contact with each other the entire time.

I wanted our relationship to be separate and my feelings and thoughts to be independent. Would the telepathic link affect me? I had to trust Vuong not to broadcast intimate thoughts and feelings. Like what Giang said, I reluctantly admitted. I had to trust her anyway. I had to trust them. The way they trusted me.

Then I wondered whether it was an effect of empathy. Other psychedelic drugs claimed astral travel, mindreading and altered consciousness. Empathy affected emotions and feelings, engendering closeness that could result in telepathy in situations such as that of the clones, I reasoned. It did not happen commonly, or it would be fake news already. Maybe when the concentration was right and the individual circumstances allowed for it, it would occur.

Now that I was close to Vuong I entertained the possibility I could be prone to telepathy through Vuong. I could be part of the clones' telepathic circle.

My first reaction was fear.

I came to myself. I was still holding Vuong's hand. Her face expressed her concern for me.

- Can you hear me?

Vuong wrapped me in an embrace but I was still alone in my thoughts.

The familiar buzz of energy I received from her being helped me regain the feelings I had for her.

"I don't share everything with the others," Vuong said. "I was individuated before I met them. I keep things to myself. Like you."

"So our relationship is private? Just us two?"

"Yes. I don't share you with them. You are just mine." She said this possessively, but I didn't mind.

I smiled at our growing rapport. Vuong was a distinct individual and perceptive enough to understand why I felt so threatened by the telepathy.

That was what I had to remember, I told myself. No matter how weird the clones got I now had this intimacy with Vuong that was ours, just ours.

To me, it was the one good thing that seemed to come from empathy.

I met Freja for a drink so I could fill her in on the clones and their research with empathy. I decided to keep the telepathy to myself. I did not want another dose of anti-psychotics.

Freja did not believe me at first. So I asked her to meet the clones. I needed her help, for someone else to know that we had a meeting with Truong and CHESS if anything went wrong. She softened a little when I told her about Vuong.

"I didn't know you played both teams," she said, smiling. "I want to meet her, for sure."

I showed her the clones' website and research and I could tell it impressed her.

We met again at my favourite coffee place. Freja's eyes darted from one clone to another, her stare widening. Vuong stood up and gave me a kiss on the cheek. The apprehension I felt at introducing Freja dissolved in my happiness at seeing Vuong again. We established the language in common was English, a second or third language for all of us.

"So you four are clones, are you?" Freja asked, sitting down. "Which one of you is the original?"

I glared at her rudeness, but the clones just laughed.

"There isn't one," Khanh said.

"Then how were you made?"

I cringed. Freja had no sensitivity at all. Perhaps it was her English that made her blunt and crude in expression.

"Artificially," Giang told her.

"And you're testers for empathy. Are they taking any more people on?"

"It's not what you think, Freja," I interjected. "They are a set of test subjects. They don't recruit them from the general public."

"But you need me to monitor what goes on when you're being tested through your phone."

"Yes, please," Vuong said softly.

"You believe in this saturation point like in the fake news?" Freja asked as our coffee and cake were served.

"It's not fake news," Khanh said flatly.

I shared her irritation and my regret at making them meet Freja rose.

"It's a bit hard to believe that Germans are influenced to do good because they've taken a party drug," Freja continued. "Maybe in Việt Nam people would do this. Or the government would do this. But not in Germany."

"Germany is not exempt. It is the home of CHESS," Khanh pointed out.

"And with your history you need empathy," Lien spoke for the first time.

As soon as her cake was finished Freja stood up to go. I walked her to the door.

"They are like a cult," Freja hissed at me. "I'll monitor your CHESS meeting over your phone. But to keep an eye on them and what they are up to. And what Truong is up to. You be careful now."

My irritation faded as I hugged her goodbye. Freja genuinely thought she was looking out for me and my interests. I couldn't stay angry at her.

When I went back to our table the clones were their normal, blasé selves again.

"Your friend is very strong-minded," Vuong said, reaching for my hand. Her familiarity eased the rest of my discomfort away.

"She cares about me," I mumbled.

"So do we," Khanh said.

"I know. I care about you all too," I replied. A warm feeling infused me and I was content and in love again.

My awkwardness with Freja was forgotten as I kissed Vuong on the cheek.

Berlin – Vuong

Kissing My restored me to myself again. I felt anchored down in the solidity of us. It was unlike we, where I shared everything as an echo of myself four times over. With My I felt separate but together, at home with me. I felt back to normal – whatever that was for me now.

My was questioning everything that occurred. She was wary of we and I didn't blame her. She was overwhelmed by the thought of our telepathy and I could not help her with it except to reassure her that I wouldn't broadcast us to we. I shared with her my initial aversion to our group mind and she seemed to take comfort in it. I understood her fear of losing herself.

I did not know what the future held for we, so I could not promise My anything.

She did not seem to mind. She was glad that we came together without empathy. She questioned her relationship with Truong, having been under the influence of the drug almost all of the time she had been with him.

"I do like you, My," I said boldly the day after we first kissed. So much could happen in a few days – I wanted to make sure she knew.

My turned an embarrassed colour as I kissed her again.

"I like you too," she muttered and then looked me in the eye. I felt a sense of connection then, with another person, another being separate to we. I felt secure in myself, with a surge of desire.

"You can come and stay with me if you get tired of being with your clone sisters," My offered.

"I'll keep that in mind," I said. I had not even considered the possibility of being apart from we. When I thought about it, I immediately felt lonely. Then I thought of My and the loneliness receded. But it was not the same. She could not shadow my every move and thought. That could be a good thing, I reflected.

My had used enough empathy to experience its medium-term effects and she exhibited no signs of telepathy. She seemed soothed from her initial fear of our telepathy, to my relief.

We were honest with each other and that had to be a good thing.

Vuong's touch was gentle, molten.

I never thought I would feel this way about a girl, but Vuong was a spunk. I admired her independence in standing up to the twins. She had a quicksilver energy to her that I wanted to touch and play with. I wanted to run my fingers over her skin and make her smile in delight.

I had to take on face value her telepathy with the other clones.

It still spooked me when the clones mirrored each other in body language. Since I kissed Vuong, though, she had stopped being in sync with them, at least when I was there.

I was glad that we went out on dates, and we did not spend a lot of time in the house where she lived. But even when we were not with them, we talked about them. I was curious about what life was like for them and for we.

Vuong knew how the others had been raised apart. They had shared the missing twenty-odd years together in the last few months.

I could not imagine what it would be like, what a shock to the system it would have been.

I felt angry on behalf of those little girls and the women they had become.

Vuong was angry, Lien was grateful and the twins were somewhere in between.

Vuong was the clone I related to the most and I felt her solidity with her touch. Her feelings ran deep and a need in me was met that Truong had never touched. That no man had ever touched. I felt I could trust her with my deepest fears and thoughts. And she would not run away.

She brought out my independence of mind and my tenderness. I could give and receive and be protective of her, she had shown me her vulnerable face while talking about Camille. And I could make it better for her, and she could for me. Our relationship did not depend on empathy and it made it more true to me.

Vuong nodded when I told her so and kissed me gently.

"We can try having no empathy," Vuong said. "I used it with Camille. Recreationally."

"Same with Truong."

We snuggled up in bed in her room.

"How are you without…"

"Alone. I am alone with you and its beautiful. Even more rare is that it is quiet in my mind without a chorus of clones eavesdropping on my thoughts."

I held her close and kissed her on the nose.

"We can get to know each other the traditional way," My suggested.

"You mean by talking and having a conversation?"

"Yes," My said, smiling.

Khanh and Giang welcomed our change of heart to be test subjects.

Truong got in contact after two days. He set up a rendez-vous with My at the CHESS facility and we could all attend. It was the best he could do.

Lien expressed her fear that they might try to detain us. My recorded the meeting with her phone, transmitting it to her friend Freja so that if anything went wrong someone outside would know and could inform the New Zealand embassy in the first instance.

Khanh and Giang had done their homework for the research protocol and knew what should happen with the next phase of the trial. They should take a sample of our blood and then inject us with the vaccine or a placebo, Giang told we.

We caught the U-Bahn to CHESS. My told us that her mother worked as a cleaner there. Perhaps Lien could work there, I suggested to My, who seemed surprised I would suggest such a thing.

At the guards' station, My provided her name and the name of a research scientist. We waited patiently for her to come. She came out in the company of a handsome, casually dressed young man. From My's reaction I knew this was Truong. I discreetly held her hand and squeezed it in sympathy.

We introduced ourselves and followed her into the brown building. We went past a reception area into a corridor that led into medical examination rooms.

"Two of you can stay here. The other two can come with me," a lab technician nodded at us.

- Khanh will stay here. I'll go to the other room with Lien, Giang said.

I elected to stay with My and Khanh. Truong stayed with us too.

"Thank you for arranging this so quickly, Truong. As you know this is time-sensitive," Khanh said. The technician put on rubber gloves and prepared the needles. There were four vials, far more than what was needed.

I tried to relax as Khanh went first. I looked away as my blood was administered.

Then the lab technician took some vials from the fridge.

"This is a blind trial, so we don't know which of you has the placebo and which of you has the drug," the technician informed us.

I tolerated the prick of the needle.

I felt past the sting of the injection. Then she gave me a second injection, in my other arm. Two injections? What for?

Khanh received her two injections. The lab technician told us to wait.

"Giang?" Khanh said aloud.

I looked up.

"Giang!" Khanh called out.

"She's not here. She's next door…" I said hurriedly.

"I'm her twin. Something's wrong. Take me to her please," Khanh asked the technician.

She shrugged and led the way to an adjacent examination room.

They opened the door and Giang rushed to Khanh's side, grabbing her hands.

Lien exchanged glances with me.

There was no telepathy from the twins.

It's lack was like a chasm opening up beneath we.

The injections had done something to their psychic ability.

Truong was watching from the sidelines. His stare made Khanh and Giang regain their composure in a hurry. They remembered what they were hiding.

"We're twins. And we feel when something is upsetting the other one," Khanh said. "You gave us two injections when the protocol is one injection only. What have you injected us with?"

Truong spread his hands.

"Your situation is unique. Anyone can trial flu vaccines. But you helped the development of empathy. What we trialled on you is a possible antidote to empathy."

Anger rose in me then. Our trust had been abused again. And we had endangered our biggest secret.

"I knew we couldn't trust you!" My spat at Truong.

"We just need to keep track of your health for the next few days," Truong said. "There should be no ill effects. We were going to test you blind to remove the placebo effect, but we can do away with that now," the lab technician added.

"No thanks," Lien said quietly. "I'm done now." She walked out of the laboratory.

We could only follow suit and back her up. My came too, furious.

Truong did not try to stop us leaving. We caught the U-Bahn back to our house.

"We can get our blood analysed and then be treated for it," Khanh suggested once we came home. "We don't have to depend on them. And we can make the antidote public property. We can defect to another multi-national chemical company. Give them our blood to sample."

Khanh and Giang were distraught and inconsolable. They held hands. They had seen the true face of the Department and their naive belief was gone.

I felt depressed – a flatness of everything around me. Lien seemed withdrawn and down. Only the twins had increased affect, but only their feelings about feeling nothing.

My was horrified at what had occurred. I could barely comfort her. My depression was so overwhelming. I could only take small reassurance in My's embrace.

Freja was stunned into silence by what had occurred. She had missed the telepathy component, only understanding that we had trialled a drug against our will. She volunteered to get some food and drink. I knew she would be thinking of alcohol and was grateful to her.

I suggested to the twins then that we try using empathy.

It may correct the effect of the antidote.

I tried not to pressure the twins to take empathy but their helplessness was amplified in we. We were so alone, deaf and blind. Everything was muted except for the panicked terror that threatened to drown we.

"Let's wait another hour," Khanh said aloud. "It might wear off by itself."

One hour went by and the twins were silent still. They were panicking, crying, and their mood affected us all. The edge of their desperation cut the rest of us like knives.

Finally, I suggested that I would take empathy first, alone. Khanh came to my side.

Lien and I took empathy. I felt the customary lift the drug gave me and the depression I had felt was shed like falling autumn leaves.

"My mood has changed. I'm back to me," I said out loud.

Lien smiled as her circumstances was restored and she gave the tablets to the twins.

"Let's try it," Khanh said.

They swallowed the tablets together.

Nothing happened at first.

- *What happens if this is permanent?* Giang asked.
- *We are here,* they both chimed in at once.

They were giddy with relief.

The antidote was easily reversible and not permanent.

I felt the elation of the twins at their restored telepathy. Then I felt their anger at the attempted blind testing, echoed by my own.

I could understand from a research point of view why they wanted to test blind, but the reality of their deception left a bad taste in my mouth. Despite Truong's words there seemed to have been no placebo delivered to any of us test subjects.

My was angry at herself for suggesting Truong. We assured her it was not her fault. She had told us his previous track record and it was equally our mistake.

I comforted her, saying that she could not have known. I was glad I had told her of our telepathy, so she knew what was going on without needing further explanations.

My knew a Vietnamese doctor at a clinic who specialised in drug use. We decided to test the content of our blood through him, through the public health system, where it could be recorded that afternoon.

Dr Mendes' clinic was in a large house in Alexanderplatz. The receptionist did a double take as we presented ourselves alongside My.

"My Nguyen, a patient, and her friends are here," she paged the doctor over the phone.

Dr Mendes came out, an older, balding man with long, white fingers. His eyes widened as he saw we.

"My friends have been given a drug that we don't know the effects of," My began.

"Really? Empathy-related?"

"An antidote to empathy."

Dr Mendes showed us to an office and shut the door. He sat down behind the desk. Giang and Khanh sat opposite him, leaving three of us standing against the walls.

"And you are quintuplets? No – quadruplets."

- His accent, he's Northern. From Hanoi. He could be from the Party.

"How were you injected with an antidote?"

"We were told it was new and it would be fun. But it's not. It's a downer. Like the comedown of the drug's after effects."

Dr Mendes leant back in his chair.

"We will get further if you tell me the truth," he said. "I'm from the North but I'm not political. What I'm interested in is the science. So I'll ask you again. Where did the antidote come from?"

"CHESS," we chorused together and took pleasure at him being taken aback.

"We want samples of our blood to be taken and analysed. Then the results to be released into the public domain," Khanh said.

"That's very commendable of you. I can order a blood array and other tests – it will take two days. But can you tell me why you want to breach your contractual confidentiality clause?"

The clones laughed.

- We signed no contract!
- What contract?

We were amused.

"So long as you understand you would never be trusted in research ever again. CHESS is jealous of its intellectual property. That includes your blood."

We laughed again.

My spread her hands out helplessly.

"They've been under a great deal of stress lately," My said.

"I'll do this for you because you are your mother's daughter. Does she know?"

"No, I don't think so…" My said and we fell silent.

"I'll treat this as if you were one of my patients. As if you all were. So I will not tell your mother. But think about telling her for my sake," the doctor said.

"In the meantime, would you like to stay here under observation just in case?" Dr Mendes said after a pause.

"Nein, Danke," I said, my first German words.

"I will call you to check on you tomorrow, just in case," he repeated, frowning.

"Thank you, Dr Mendes," My said softly.

"Yes, thank you. We do appreciate it. Please quote us a fee and we will meet it," I said. Dr Mendes meant well. It was not his fault that his terms of reference for human ethical behaviour with CHESS were at odds with ours.

We went back to our house, expecting to be apprehended at any moment.

We were anxious at first that the Department would come after us. But no one contacted us. Not even Truong.

This made we suspicious. We wondered about Dr Mendes and whether he was connected to the black market and Truong. But it was too late to recall what we had given him.

Two days went by with no contact from anyone. My did two shifts at her restaurant and we explored Berlin's museums. The exhibitions were vast but cold. German museums contained monuments from other eras like the Roman Empire, stolen from their home countries. German modern art was discordant to we.

My and I went out for dinner together. My took me to a restaurant bar. I felt freer without the clones nearby. I did not have to maintain a wall in front of my thoughts. I could just relax in the privacy of my mind. It was a relief.

As we sat down and ordered drinks, I felt a joy in being normal, just another girl on a date. And I could forget about Camille.

We talked about our childhoods. My was ordinary, born and bred in Berlin. She felt sad for me not having had we until now.

"But it must be wonderful being back together now," My commented.

"It is. I feel complete now. But they can be a bit much sometimes. I'm glad of my independence of mind."

"I'm glad you stand apart from them too. I would not be with you otherwise," My told me honestly.

"It makes me wonder whether the Department had the right idea in separating us at five. They didn't have to segregate us overseas, but they could have still had us brought up with different families in Hanoi and allowed us to meet earlier."

"What you went through was horrible," My said softly. "I'm amazed that you still wish to help out."

"It's our duty and purpose," I found myself saying. My sense of responsibility to the community and the world in general had increased since being in Berlin. I had been influenced by we.

"What do you think about the saturation point?" My asked.

"It's done. There's nothing we can do about it. We live with the consequences," I said. I neglected to say that most of we thought it was a good thing. The way things were, My was already alienated from the clones enough.

"I wonder why they think we need an antidote for empathy," My wondered.

"In case they need another war," I said light-heartedly, then stopped, realising what I had said.

My took a sip of her wine.

"I hope not," she replied.

Dr Mendes called us two days later to explain to us that the drug was a powerful mood stabiliser. This made sense for an empathy antidote. He thanked us for bringing the drug to him – it could help people too affected by empathy-like substances.

Perhaps we should have been more suspicious.

We did not hear from the Department at all, and we did not wish to draw attention to ourselves. Khanh and Giang monitored the research database from CHESS and discovered that our blood sample results had somehow made their way to CHESS in Berlin and the Department in Việt Nam the same day we received the results.

We surmised that Dr Mendes had forwarded the test results on to CHESS in Berlin and the Department in Hanoi. For science. He may have informed them that he had the sample and we to test. Being tested in Berlin rather than by the Department in Việt Nam meant that results could be shared with CHESS almost immediately. It also meant the blood samples could be worked on in labs in Berlin rather than in Việt Nam, we realised.

Whatever we did, the Vietnamese government, CHESS or the Department got what they wanted. Even in Berlin. My life had been controlled by them all along. It was foolish of me to believe any different.

The only action I had taken of my own free will had been my liaison with My. For which I was thankful. It made being stranded in Berlin tolerable for me.

The reason for our very existence was research.

Khanh and Giang wrote an article about it to release on the internet.

"You can't trust anyone," Khanh said.

"They have left us alone," Lien commented.

"Maybe they've realised we're better off acting as free agents," she added.

"This is what we wanted to see happen in the first place," Giang pointed out.

- *Everything we do plays into their hands,* I said. I felt depressed when I was not angry at how we had been played out by the Department and CHESS.

I would never be free of them.

- *We still have we,* said Lien.

I was reminded that to Lien any life outside detention was better. Things could be worse for her. For we.

I had a new relationship to occupy me.

- *And we are free in Berlin,* Khanh pointed out.

That there was an antidote to empathy seemed like news to we. We posted it and the followers that believed empathy was in the water grabbed onto it immediately. It was labelled fake news and discredited before we had even begun.

If empathy had assisted compliance in the taking up of vaccines, surely this was a good thing, Khanh would argue. Muddying the waters still further by questioning people's willingness to adapt to the practices and empathy's influence on them may only do harm.

With My, she had drip-fed information about the clones and empathy for months and was increasingly frustrated by the lack of serious engagement she was receiving. She had had enough of fake news on the dangers of 5G and QAnon.

That knowledge made no net difference to people's behaviour.

No one else noticed any difference.

Our blood test results were used to tweak a formula for the antidote. Now they had our blood samples, work was started almost immediately in labs in Berlin. CHESS was efficient in its research, we had to give it that.

Some good had to come of all this.

I went home in a daze. I felt so bad about what I had inadvertently put into play for the clones. Once I was in the familiar comfort of my bedroom, the despair I felt sloughed off me like a rain shower. Instead, I felt the inner glow that I associated with good sex. Vuong had awoken desire in me again – without chemical empathy.

I was relieved and grateful. It felt natural, as if it was meant to be.

I was falling in love for real this time, I thought.

I hopped onto the computer and opened up the fake news sites that I had monitored for mention of empathy and cloning. There was nothing new, just exclamations of surprise. There was always someone to which the content was news.

At least I could enhance what is going on in my own small way, I thought.

I could still tell the truth and people would listen, and maybe if I was lucky true influencers would believe. I had exposed Truong and made Freja at least think twice about trusting him over me.

I could not tell my mother about the clones. She would want me back in the hospital with Dr Mendes. He would be used to keeping secrets when it suited him, I thought. I could protect my mother with ignorance of the Department and CHESS.

I was happy to provide and monitor content for the multiples in the meantime. For Vuong.

The clones were all smart women, although a bit eccentric. I started releasing the scientific data that Khanh and Giang had provided me with. It made interesting reading.

What the Department and government were up to with their tests and empathy research sounded just like more fake news conspiracies. Only actually meeting the clones had convinced me there were multiples.

All I could do now was try to convince others virtually.

I started researching other multi-national pharmaceutical companies. There were many for us to choose from if we would chose to share all of the CHESS research we knew about. I wondered whether the multiples would willingly sell their services as trial participants. Somehow, I doubted that.

I could serve my purpose by serving theirs, as well as by spreading news about empathy and the saturation point.

I could still be useful and do my best for Vuong.

Berlin – Vuong

As for we…

Evelyn contacted we a day later. She came alone and I wanted to slam the door in her face when she appeared on our doorstep.

The others let her in.

- *Let's see what she has to say,* Khanh said.

"I'm here to apologise for misleading you. It was not well done, and I would have spoken out against it had I known. We should work with you, not against you." I sensed anger, then great anger, and I realised how little power Evelyn actually had. She was just a monitor, not a decision-maker.

"I don't blame you if you don't trust me or don't talk to me. They sent me to Berlin especially to see if we can get you back."

"What do they want?" asked Lien.

"To continue monitoring you and running regular blood tests. They don't want to put you under house arrest, although the Department could arrest Lien. They'd prefer you all to be voluntary. And to not sell out to another multi-national. Whatever you've been offered, CHESS will beat it."

We had only been researching multi-nationals. We had not decided on which one to approach or even whether we would sell ourselves as test subjects yet. Evelyn's assumption spoke of the limitations and bias of their surveillance in Berlin.

"And if they want psych tests and accurate blood responses to empathy, we can't be under too much stress or it will skew the findings," I said suddenly. I could see a way out of our stalemate with the Department. We could still fulfil our purpose outside the Department. If I had learnt anything from the last few months, it was the efficiency of the CHESS research arm. The production of vaccines was unprecedented in its speed. They had questionable ethics in their recruitment of test participants but there was no question about the usefulness of the results, empathy- and flu-related. And maybe we could be part of it, after all, and help without compromising our freedom and safety.

If we could trust them again.

"Let us be free in Berlin and we will do your blood tests with Dr Mendes," I proposed to Evelyn.

- *What do you think?* I asked Giang and Khanh simultaneously.
- *Well, it's true,* Khanh said. *We would have skewed blood-work from the adrenaline and cortisol flooding our systems. And they'd know this now. We can preserve Lien's freedom.*

Evelyn looked at us one after the other.

"I know I can take your word for it. But my superiors may not trust your good will. They would want you to stop spamming the internet about the saturation point."

- *It's already out on the internet. It cannot be covered up,* Giang commented.

"We can stop our social media posts," Vuong said.

- *My will continue,* Khanh reminded we.
- *Let people have the empathy information on faith that if someone needed to know the truth they would know where to find it.*

"You've already released into the public domain the information that is useful for the Department," Evelyn continued. "Your timing was perfect."

- *Timing?*

"Your defection to Berlin and the release of your research information on the internet helped the Department. We wanted to release our findings into the public domain to further refine empathy, but CHESS wanted the research patented and commercial in confidence, with only its own scientists working on it. You leaking the information on the internet forced them to be patent-free so we all could work on the research without restriction. The Department could not be seen to be leaking information deliberately against protocol. So the Department thanks you for doing that."

We received this news in silence.

- It was too easy for us to go to Berlin. Now we knew why.
Khanh was disgusted.
- They seemed to have anticipated our every move. All we could do was play along. Pretend like we meant it.

"How can we trust that the Department won't try to inject something else into our veins?" I asked, returning to the matter at hand. I veered off, thinking too much about Evelyn's revelation for the time being.

Evelyn looked away before answering.

"You can bring witnesses. Not just your German girlfriend. Anyone you like."

Evelyn looked at me. I was aghast and drew in a breath to speak.

- Do not let her get to you, Giang said in my head and I exhaled, my words unspoken.
- Leave My out of this.

"We will provide you with the information about any substance you take. You won't need to look it up anymore," she said to Giang. "And you'll only have to deal with Dr Mendes and me from now on. Would that be all right by you?"

Evelyn had pre-empted our possible objections dealing with the Department and CHESS. We'd only deal with people we were familiar with, like Evelyn and Dr Mendes in the Alexanderplatz clinic.

"It would keep your stress hormone levels down," she said.

We let Evelyn go with the promise that Dr Mendes would contact us in a couple of days, giving us some time to think about it. She confirmed our suspicions about the doctor who had provided our results to both CHESS and the Department, which provided little comfort. At least we knew he was interested in science, regardless of national and corporate boundaries.

But I was assured by them sending Evelyn to talk to us and accompany us. They were not going to strongarm us again. Not if they wanted useful data from us – and the empathy research was worth millions.

They needed we free and willing in Berlin, so I thought.

Evelyn promised that Lien would not be prosecuted. She did not mention My again. I wanted to threaten non–co-operation if they dragged her into this, but Giang cautioned me to not mention her at all.

We knew the best thing we could do for ourselves now was to live out our ordinary lives in Berlin. The truth was out there for people who wished to find it on the internet.

Lien was still free.

Our test results were being used in the development of a novel influenza vaccine.

I wondered whether my feeling of wanting to do good via CHESS regardless of threats to My was influenced by empathy. The twins in particular seemed to have forgotten the Department's betrayal of their trust. They were genuinely altruistic in their actions.

Even when our flight to Berlin played into the Department's hands, I still wished to contribute to their research. If this was the long-term effect of empathy, this benign motivation, compassion and forgiveness, it was frighteningly effective.

Did it matter, when the desired result was the same?

We were empathy. We could work with CHESS for the greater good. No matter how we reached that point, it had to be worth it.

The effects of empathy on we affected the world.

And My and me.

Berlin – My

I touched the surface of the mirror with my fingers and silently greeted my reflection. The cute girl with black hair and bird-bright eyes smiled back at me.

I knew we were being monitored so I did not speak aloud.

Dr Mendes knocked on the door of my room and I let him in with a nod.

"How are we today?" he asked.

"Fine," I replied. I thought he was using a figure of speech rather than referring to we. I hadn't told him about we.

At least I didn't think so.

People would think I was crazy if I did.

"Are you expecting Truong to visit today?" he asked.

"Yes."

"And Truong is…"

"My boyfriend." And an empathy dealer. I kept this to myself also.

Dr Mendes was testing me. If I answered all his questions correctly, I would get to go home. That meant no mention of multiples or the saturation point.

I knew what sounded improbable and delusional and what made sense.

I knew what was normal now the anti-psychotics had taken effect.

"How's your mother?"

"She's fine," I replied.

"What will you do once you are discharged?" he asked.

"Go back to study."

"Do you remember what you told me yesterday? About clones?"

"Oh, I know they don't exist today," I said light-heartedly. "Not for humans yet."

Dr Mendes smiled at me.

"You may be ready to go home in a day or two," he said.

I saw him out the door.

I looked in the mirror and we smiled at we.

We were ready to leave and be free to be.

Hoa Pham

Acknowledgements

Thank you to the Goethe Institut in Berlin, the Literaturwerksttat and Western Sydney University for my inspirational residency in Berlin in 2009. Thank you to Pham Thi Hoai, Lady Gaby, Kate Davison and Archana Prassad for showing me Berlin.

Thank you to Varuna Writers Centre for space and support to write. Thank you to Larissa Lai and Gold SF for their work and faith.

As always thank you to my alpha readers Anna Mandoki, Liz Kemp, and Margaret Bearman. And to someone whom I can never thank enough Alister Air who is still waiting for our ship to come in.